Bourbon & Bordeaux

A SMALL TOWN STEAMY ROMANCE

WELCOME TO KISSING SPRINGS
BOOK THREE

JOI JACKSON

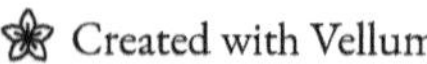 Created with Vellum

Prologue

"Thank you for calling The Book Barrel, Kentucky's best-kept secret for local bourbon and literature. We are unavailable to take your call, but please leave a message, and we'll get back to you as soon as possible. Please visit our website to order your favorite books or to join our mailing list. Have a bookish day!"

"Hi, this message is for Saxon Mitchell. Mr. Mitchell, as you probably know by now, since I've called and left numerous messages, texts, emails, and faxes, this is Lovie Whitfield, again, hoping to talk with you about an exclusive book signing at your store for Sloane St. James. I'm sure you have my number as I leave it each time I talk to your voicemail, but here it is again, along with my email, lovie at loviewhitfieldPR.com. As always, I look forward to hearing from you soon. Thank you!

"Hey, Lovie Whitfield again from Lovie Whitfield Public Relations. God, that's kind of a mouthful when you say it quickly. Anyway, would love to talk to you about a book signing for Sloane. She's in talks with Good Morning America, and if we can coordinate the signing at The Book Barrel with her interview, we'd all benefit. Please call me back, thanks!"

"Mr. Mitchell, why won't you call me back? Please call, text, or email. Hell, you can even fax me. This is Lovie. You know that already."

"Lovie Whitfield leaving yet another message... you know, at this point, I'm talking to myself. Clearly you have zero interest in working with me, and that's fine. It would have been nice if you'd just said so, but message received loud and clear. I'll quit pestering you now. Have a nice life, Saxon Mitchell."

"Okay, one more try. Saxon, this is Lovie again. Look, I'm sorry if I came off rude in the last message. I just don't understand why you won't return my calls. I really think you're missing out on an amazing opportunity here. Reese Witherspoon says Sloane's book is the new *Eat, Pray, Love*. Can we please talk? Just one quick phone call? All right...I hope to hear from you, but if not, I wish you the best. Goodbye, Saxon."

"I have to assume these calls are not going to a landline but your direct cell, and you're choosing to ignore them, Mr. Mitchell. I WILL NOT BE IGNORED! Okay, maybe that was a bit much. I'm not going to boil your rabbit or anything. If Google is listening, I'm just kidding! These are jokes. Anyway, would love to hear from you. You know who this is by now. Bye."

CHAPTER 1
Saxon

Saxon opened the door to The Book Barrel and inhaled the comforting, familiar aroma of old and new books that lined the walls. With each step he took, he felt himself relax in the serenity of his bookstore. He missed this place.

With a sigh of contentment, Saxon walked up and down the aisles of his store taking in all its wonders. Here, he could go on long journeys just by reading stories from authors both old and new, without leaving his beloved establishment.

Saxon paused, taking the store in. His trip to Ghana for a business venture that ended up not panning out quite as planned had taken him from the store for a full month. Now, however, things were finally back to normal; it was just him and his books once more, and it felt good.

There was a lot to catch up on, he knew, but for now he was content to roam through The Book Barrel's timeless collection of stories waiting to be read by their next owner. No matter what happened outside, his bookstore would always be waiting for him.

As Saxon made his way to his office, his phone chimed, indicating a new message. Saxon groaned inwardly, knowing that it was probably Lovie Whitfield from Lovie Whitfield Public Relations once again.

Rolling his eyes skyward, he sighed. How many times had she said her name and the name of her company? He got it already.

He pressed the button on his phone and listened to the messages, one after the other. Lovie's voice was persistent, even slightly frantic, as she left message after message about hosting a book signing event for her client, Sloane St. James.

Saxon pursed his lips. He'd read the book—a debut self-help about relationships—and had no desire to host a signing in his store.

Despite himself, Saxon had to chuckle at the last voice mail from Lovie Whitfield.

Saxon had unplugged for the past thirty days and had taken no calls outside of emergencies, which, thankfully, there hadn't been any, and logged out of social media.

As much as he tried to ignore them, her messages still piqued his interest. He had never met the woman, but her voice was captivating, deep and sexy, and her strange sense of humor even more so.

She was persistent, if nothing else. He ran a hand over his beard and grimaced. He needed a trim. He probably looked like he'd spent the last month living in the wild. Maybe this weekend, he could slip out of the store and get one.

No time right now.

He was getting his store, The Book Barrel, ready for the evening's private event. Once a month, the older men of Kissing Springs, Kentucky, gathered at the bookstore to drink bourbon and talk about a young adult novel they read.

The book club's pick for this month was *The Hate U Give* by Angie Thomas. The men would watch the movie adaptation of it in the media room after the discussion.

Saxon made sure all the bourbon glasses were set up in flights and that he had plenty of bottles of whatever they were tasting ready for purchase.

Book club nights were a lot of work, and while he'd never admit it to anyone, he loved them. The men were reading books about young people and learning new perspectives through literature. They were relating to their grandkids and sharing stories both generations could enjoy.

It was beautiful to watch, he reflected, as he wiped down a table where a charcuterie board lay covered in plastic wrap.

As Saxon arranged the board and a tray of cookies on the table, he heard the bell above the door chime. He looked up, his eyes widening as a tall, curvy woman with flawless skin the color of dark chocolate strode in, her warm brown eyes landing on his. She looked like she didn't belong in Kissing Springs.

Saxon watched, mesmerized, as she glided across the room. She was dressed in a tight-fitting, sleeveless black dress that hugged every curve and a pair of black stilettos that accentuated her long legs.

She had to be Lovie.

He quickly tried to compose himself and then greeted her with the smile he used for new customers.

Lovie Whitfield looked even better in person than he imagined.

He'd been tempted to put her name in a search engine and see exactly what she looked like, what she was about, but he resisted that urge.

He wasn't going to agree to the signing. No sense in getting to know her.

"Hi, can I help you?" Saxon asked, wiping his hands on a towel.

"Hello, Saxon. I'm Lovie Whitfield. I was beginning to think you didn't exist," Lovie said dryly, her perfectly manicured hand resting on her hip.

"I exist," Saxon said, his tone clipped. "I just don't have any interest in a book signing with Sloane."

Lovie's face fell. "Really? Sloane St. James is trending all over social media. It would be a great opportunity for your store."

Saxon shook his head. "Not interested."

"I came all this way. You could at least hear me out."

Saxon continued to adjust the tray of cookies, avoiding eye contact. She had a slight Southern drawl, and he wanted to ask where she was from but resisted. No sense encouraging her. He had made up his mind about the signing, and no one, especially not this smoky-voiced siren, was going to talk him out of it. "I didn't ask you to come," he said finally. "Not my fault you can't take a hint."

Lovie's eyes narrowed as she regarded Saxon. "You know, you might be the first bookstore owner I've ever met who turned down a book signing with a successful author."

Saxon shrugged. "I'm not like other bookstore owners."

Lovie snorted softly, her full lips curving into a smile. "Clearly."

There was a charged silence between them as they stared at each other. Saxon couldn't deny the attraction he felt toward Lovie. Something about her confidence and the way she carried herself drew him in. He mentally shook himself. He needed to focus on the book club event.

He cleared his throat. "I really need to get back to work. I'm prepping for a book club meeting tonight," Saxon said, gesturing toward the charcuterie board.

Lovie's eyes flickered over the board and then back to him. "Mind if I stick around and browse your collection?"

Saxon hesitated. He didn't really want Lovie hanging around, but he couldn't exactly say no to a customer. "Sure, you've got about fifteen minutes before the store closes and the event starts."

Lovie beamed and began walking through the aisles, her stilettos clicking on the hardwood floors. Saxon watched her browse the shelves of books and the bourbon on display, his eyes lingering on her curvy figure. He knew he shouldn't be thinking about her like that, but he couldn't help himself.

The door chimed again, and Duke, the town's mail carrier, strolled in, a battered paperback copy of the book under his arm. Tall and lanky with ocean blue eyes and more hair on his face than his head, Duke was the reason they'd started the book club.

"Action Saxon! You get my special reserve in yet?" he asked, then stopped when he spied Lovie. "Who is that? My next ex-wife?"

Saxon rolled his eyes at Duke's comment and tried to ignore the prickle of awareness he felt as Lovie meandered through the store. "That's Lovie Whitfield. She's a PR person trying to get me to host a book signing with the one and only Sloane St. James."

The older man grunted. "Don't do it. Nothing but trouble, that one." He leaned in close, tilting his round head toward Lovie's direction. "So, is she single?"

Saxon shrugged. He hadn't seen a ring, but he would not share the fact that he'd looked for one with Duke. "You'll have to ask her."

Lovie strode back to the checkout area, a stack of children's books in her arms. She nodded a greeting at Duke. "Sorry to interrupt, but I want to get these before you kick me out."

Duke smirked. "You're welcome to stay for our meeting. We could use a woman's perspective."

Saxon let out a long sigh. "Duke, you were adamant when you started this book club that this was a space for men only. What happened to that steadfast rule?"

Duke rubbed his chin thoughtfully for a moment. "Well, Saxon, times are changing, and so should we." He gestured toward Lovie. "We'd be lucky to have an intelligent woman's opinion on the books we read and discuss."

Lovie chuckled. "That's very kind of you, but I should get going. Thank you for letting me browse your store, Saxon."

After paying for her purchases, Lovie gathered her bags.

Saxon nodded, relieved that she was leaving. "No problem. Have a good evening."

As they watched Lovie leave, Duke shook his head. "Man, you got no game. A woman like that walks in here, and you don't even try to get her number?"

"I have her number," he said with a shrug. "She called and left it a dozen times while I was gone."

Duke whistled low. "Well, seeing as how she keeps trying to

reach you, maybe you should take the hint." He winked and grabbed a cookie from the tray.

The other men continued to trickle in, wandering around the store, books or tablets in hand, ready to eat and drink while discussing *The Hate U Give*. Saxon set out the charcuterie board and poured glasses of bourbon for each of them. As he poured, his mind wandered back to Lovie's proposal as the men settled into their seats.

Duke, the unofficial MC for the group, cleared his throat. "I think most of you missed her, but Saxon here has a new admirer. She's tall like one of those models, but not all thin and wasting away."

"I got here early. I saw her in the children's section." Fletch Jackson whistled. "That black dress...and she bent over at one point... man, I almost fell over."

Saxon rubbed his temples. "You all have daughters her age. Stop it. She's not an admirer. She's a publicist that Sloane hired for her book tour. Sloane wants to have a signing here."

Duke's eyes flashed. "You told her hell no, right?"

"I did, but something tells me that's not the last we'll see of her."

Saxon's uncle, Charlie Mitchell, normally content to let the other men squabble during their meetings, spoke up. "Saxon, don't let that woman back in your life. She's nothing but trouble. You've found peace here, and Sloane will destroy it if you let her."

Out of all Saxon's extended family, his uncle Charlie was his favorite, and he normally welcomed the older man's wisdom, but they weren't here to rehash his dumpster fire of a marriage. "Thanks, Unc. Let's get this meeting going, shall we?"

Saxon walked the men through the bourbon tasting, relishing in the way the rich, amber liquid swirled in the glasses. He explained the unique qualities of the new batch he'd just added to his collection. The men listened attentively, enjoying the spirit and the camaraderie.

As they sipped their bourbons, Saxon felt a sense of pride in the community he had built in Kissing Springs, his hometown. The men gathered around him were all so different, but they shared a common love for good books and great bourbon.

He glanced over at his uncle, who was nodding approvingly and a sense of gratitude washed over him. Uncle Charlie was a constant source of support and guidance throughout Saxon's life, and he was grateful to have him here tonight.

As they finished the tasting, Saxon cleared his throat. "I'll let you gentlemen do your discussion. Let me know what I can pour for you, and then I'll get the movie cued up downstairs."

Saxon hung around for a few minutes more refilling glasses and answering questions about the bourbon he'd introduced.

The men had a heated discussion about the themes of police brutality and racial injustice in *The Hate U Give*. Saxon was proud that they'd chosen to read the book and step into the shoes of an African-American teenager grappling with the death of her friend by police hands.

After the discussion, the men retired to the media room to watch the movie adaptation of the book.

The media room was a cozy enclave tucked away in the lower level of the bookstore. Saxon had spared no expense in creating a space that was both comfortable and functional. The room looked like a classic movie theater, with three rows of plush leather recliners and a large projection screen hanging at the front.

The walls were painted a deep maroon which added to the cozy feel of the space. There were several vintage movie posters framed and hung on the walls featuring classics like *Shaft*, *Coffy* and *Uptown Saturday Night*.

A state-of-the-art sound system filled the room with crisp, clear audio. The bass was deep and immersive making the movie-watching experience more enjoyable. The lighting in the room was subtle and warm, adding to the overall ambiance.

The men settled into their seats as Saxon dimmed the lights and pressed play on the movie. The room was filled with the sounds of gunfire and shouting as the opening scene of *The Hate*

U Give played out on the screen. He watched as his friends became completely engrossed in the movie, their faces reflecting the emotions that were playing out on the screen.

For the next two hours, they were transported into the world of the book, experiencing the story in a way that only film could provide.

Saxon sat in his recliner, his thoughts again wandering to Lovie. He knew he shouldn't be thinking about her, especially since he had no interest in hosting Sloane's book signing, but he couldn't seem to shake her from his mind.

As the credits rolled, the men bid each other goodnight and headed out of the store. Saxon locked up and turned off the lights before heading to his apartment above the store.

He passed Sloane's book laying on his kitchen table. He grimaced as he passed it, and wondered why he hadn't burned it as soon as he'd read it.

CHAPTER 2

Lovie

L ovie shoved open the door of her hotel room and dumped her bags on the small, stiff sofa near the window. The hotel was an international chain, popular in small towns, with clean, basic rooms and everything she needed during her stay in Kissing Springs.

Eager to get out of her shoes, she kicked the sleek stilettos off and reached for the fuzzy socks in her bag.

She wiggled her toes after she put the socks on. Much better.

The smart black dress came off next, followed by the shapewear that smoothed and propped everything up where it needed to be. Opening the closet, Lovie carefully hung what she considered to be one of her best dresses. She might need to don it again sometime during the trip.

Only when she was in her favorite sleep shirt, an oversized Howard University t-shirt that had seen better days, did she consider her day.

Yes, she'd managed to corner Saxon Mitchell in his store, which she had to admit, was beautiful and not at all what she'd expected to find in a small Southern town in Kentucky.

The basic website, with a few images of the storefront and the bourbon bar, hadn't done the store or the man justice.

Lovie picked up the bag of books she'd purchased for her young nieces back in Charlotte. Saxon carried a surprisingly diverse selection of children's books, and she knew her nieces would love them.

Saxon Mitchell.

He wasn't what she'd expected at all.

Before making the drive to Kissing Springs from her home in Charlotte, Lovie had looked Saxon up online. Everything she found centered on his bookstore; there was very little personal information about the owner.

But in person, Saxon had been a surprise. She hadn't realized he was so tall. She was five-nine, closer to six feet in her heels, and she still had to look up at him.

She'd noted that the glasses he wore in the promo pictures on his website were absent when she met him, allowing her to experience those piercing, deep brown eyes of his. As soon as Saxon realized who she was, his gaze had gone from appreciation to annoyance.

Lovie expected him to be a typical bookstore owner: absent-minded, geeky, awkward. Saxon checked none of those boxes. He was broad-shouldered, sharp, and wasn't afraid to speak his mind. She'd gotten the sense he was seconds away from politely tossing her out.

Lovie assumed the little black dress would get his attention, then she'd close the deal while he was distracted, but she'd underestimated him. Lovie knew she needed to come up with a new plan, something that would convince Saxon to change his mind.

Lovie's mind worked as she folded herself into the chair at the writing desk next to the sofa. She couldn't let this opportunity slip away. Sloane St. James was on the brink of celebrity status, and if Lovie pulled off this book tour, maybe she could ride Sloane's coattails to turn her fledgling public relations business around.

Her phone rang as she searched the website for the small town. She smiled as she swiped to answer the call.

"Auntie Love, are you sure you're gonna be home from 'Tucky for my birthday?"

Lovie bit her lip to keep from chuckling at her five-year-old niece, Jasmine. "It's Kentucky, sweetheart, and yes, I will be back in plenty of time for your birthday."

"Okay, you promised to make me into a princess." There was a rustling noise, and she heard what she feared was Jasmine dropping the phone. "Mommy, I was gonna ask her, but you interrupted me."

More rustling.

"Jasmine, put that back. And give me my phone, please."

Her sister, Layla, came on the line. "Lovie? You there?"

"In full control of those kids as always, I see," Love teased.

"Girl... you are always welcome to come take them off my hands, especially the bossy one." Layla sighed. "So, you made it to Kissing Falls, or whatever that small town is, I assume?"

"Kissing Springs, and yes, I'm in my hotel room," she said, moving back to the bed and leaning against the pillows. "But the mission was a bust. He shut me down pretty much as soon as I walked into the place. Oh, I got books for the girls."

"Thanks, we need more bedtime stories. So, what happened? I thought you were gonna wear that dress I picked out? Hold on. Jeneva, don't tease your sister. Pick up your shoes and tell Jas to pick hers up, too."

Lovie grinned, shaking her head. This was typically how phone conversations with her older sister went. "Shouldn't they be in bed by now?"

"Not quite yet. Jas has been worrying me to call you to make sure you had Mr. Dream, so you wouldn't be alone in 'Tucky."

Lovie glanced over at the small furry brown stuffed bear her niece had presented to her while she packed her car for the trip. "Yep, got him, but she got on the phone asking if I was going to be back for her birthday party."

"That's because I told her she didn't need to confirm your commitment to princess her up each time she talks to you. She thinks she's slick." Lovie practically heard her sister's eye roll through the phone. "Anyway, what happened?"

"I wore the dress! Girl, I had my boobs propped up and my finest stilettos on and I walked in like I owned the place, full of confidence and Black Girl Magic. And he still said no."

"Maybe he doesn't like women?"

Lovie snorted. "Oh, I'm pretty certain he likes women. As soon as he found out I was the woman that's been stalking him for weeks, he shut down. He wanted to toss me out of his store."

"Well, if he's not into the dress, maybe you should try something else? Have you considered trying to appeal to his literary taste?"

Lovie thought about it. Saxon was a bookstore owner, after all. Maybe he had a soft spot for a particular author. She snapped her fingers. She knew what she needed to do. "I'm going back tomorrow. New plan."

"Girl, good luck. Call me and let me know how it goes. I gotta go herd these two little cats of mine to bed."

Lovie ended the call and sat back down in front of her laptop. A new plan of attack was just what she needed.

At noon the next day, Lovie strode into The Book Barrel with gifts and a grand plan.

Saxon wasn't manning the check-out counter, and she looked around hoping to see him. A serious young man who looked to be in his early twenties asked her if she needed help.

"Yes, is Saxon here? And where can I put these?" She held up a container of cupcakes. "These are for the staff."

The man's eyes lit up. "I'll take care of those. Mr. S is back in his office. I'll show you where it is."

As he led her back to Saxon's office, Lovie saw some shelves of books she'd missed the night before and vowed to come back and check them out before she left.

She knocked on the door of Saxon's office and waited for him to acknowledge her. When he did, she walked into the room, ignoring the bookshelves lining the walls. Saxon was sitting at his desk, typing away at his computer, but he looked up when she entered.

"No CFM dress and shoes today, Ms. Whitfield?" Saxon said, his voice full of disapproval as he narrowed his eyes and crossed his arms. "Answer's still no."

She frowned at him, not sure what he meant by CFM. Then, the meaning of the acronym hit her, and she stared at him in disbelief.

Come fuck me.

She opened her mouth to protest but decided against it; arguing with him would only prove his point.

He raised a brow as if challenging her, daring her to deny it. But Lovie would not give him the satisfaction; she wouldn't let him see he had rattled her. Instead, she straightened her shoulders and lifted her chin in defiance.

"I came with a peace offering," Lovie said, placing a bottle of bourbon on his desk. "This is single barrel and very exclusive. Made here in Kentucky."

He picked up the heavy amber bottle, studied it, then placed it gently back on the desk. "Impressive. But you wasted your money if you think this will persuade me to host that signing."

She huffed in frustration, crossing her arms. "You know, I traveled all the way here from Charlotte because you refused to acknowledge any of the voicemails, emails, texts and DMs that I've sent you. The least you can do is tell me why you won't even consider the book signing."

He regarded her with those mesmerizing deep brown eyes, and Lovie felt a warmth race through her. "Have you read the book?"

Shit. She didn't want to answer because she knew where this was going. "Yes."

Saxon continued to stare. "The entire book?"

"Yes."

"And what did you think of it?"

Shit. Shit. Shit. "I normally don't read self-help books, so it wasn't my cup of tea." Technically, she hadn't lied.

He tented his fingers, leaning back in his chair. "Fair enough. What do you normally read?"

She shrugged. "Mysteries, thrillers, and romance. Not necessarily in that order. Why?"

"I've owned this store for almost five years now. I've learned to read people, excuse the pun, and I can normally sense what they like." Lovie waited as he continued to study her like she was an object on a display shelf. "I'm willing to bet you didn't like the book, and it has nothing to do with it being self-help."

She turned away, refusing to admit anything. She'd only skimmed the book before she'd signed a contract with Sloane's publishing company. Once the contract was a done deal, she'd set aside time to read it, and he was right. She'd hated it.

He chuckled. "Your silence speaks volumes, Ms. Whitfield."

Lovie tensed, feeling her cheeks heat. She couldn't deny Saxon's intuition, but she also didn't want to admit that she'd signed on to promote a book she didn't enjoy. It was a rookie mistake she wouldn't make again.

She turned back to face him, her arms still crossed over her chest. "So what if I didn't like the book? I am not her ideal reader. However, I still think it's a great opportunity for your store. And for your customers."

Saxon shook his head. "I'm sure her ideal readers are not my ideal customers."

She sighed. She needed to tell him everything. This was her last chance. "I'm sure you can't relate to this, but the call from Sloane's publisher came at just the right moment."

She flopped in the seat across from his desk, staring at the abstract art on the wall behind him. "I lost my job as a public relations specialist for a non-profit that lost funding and had to close last year. While I've been saving up to branch out on my own, it was rough going, and I basically started this firm because I wanted to bet on myself. But I had to spend a lot of my savings on day-to-day expenses, and I'm helping my sister out as she's going through a nasty divorce... anyway, I said all that to say I was about to throw in the towel and start looking for any job I could find when they called me asking if I could promote her book tour."

Lovie hated to bare her soul, but she had no choice. "This money will help me get back on my feet and will hopefully open more doors to more clients. But their stipulation is that this store kicks off the tour. I understand she lived here for a while?"

Saxon's expression darkened, and Lovie's heart pounded. What had she said to elicit his anger?

She sat, watching him as he ran his hand over his forehead.

Unable to bear the silence any longer, Lovie blurted. "I've said too much, haven't I?"

Saxon rose. "It's too early for a stiff drink," he muttered. "You up for a walk? There's a coffee shop a couple blocks from here."

The shift in his demeanor unnerved her. "Umm...sure, I saw that place on my way here."

He nodded, grabbing a jacket from a coat rack in the corner. "Let's go."

Lovie followed Saxon out of the store, feeling a mix of confusion and relief. She couldn't read his expression, but she was grateful he didn't ask her any more questions about the book. As they walked down the tree-lined street, she tried to focus on the scenery to distract herself from the tension between them.

When they reached the coffee shop, Saxon held the door open for her, then approached the cashier.

"Hey, John, can I get a large black coffee and," he motioned to the menu, "whatever she wants?"

Lovie only drank coffee when she needed to be alert, and she sensed she'd need to be sharp around Saxon. "Just a small cappuccino, please."

After Saxon paid for their order, they took their drinks and found a small table in the corner. Saxon said nothing at first, just sipped his coffee. Finally, he spoke. "She did live here for a while, but she hated it. Sloane St. James is my ex-wife."

Lovie was mid-sip and nearly dropped her cup when he dropped that little nugget on her. "What?"

She blinked at him, unable to comprehend his words. "The publisher didn't tell me that..."

He nodded. "I'm not surprised. We've been divorced for two years now."

Lovie set her cup down, her mind reeling. Realization dawned on her. "Was she talking about you when she described taming her husband?"

"That fucking book." He balled his hand into a fist, and Lovie expected him to bang the table. "There's stuff in there I confided in her, and she's using it for financial gain."

Her hand covering her mouth, Lovie said more to herself than Saxon, "God, no wonder you didn't respond to my calls."

A million questions bubbled up in her. "Why is she so adamant about hosting a book signing at your store?"

Saxon sipped his coffee. "My store was recently profiled as one of the hottest Black-owned bookstores in the country, whatever that means, so that could be it. Sloane may be looking to capitalize off that. But there's also a chance she's doing this to spite me. Our divorce was messy and contentious. She may try to make a statement by having her book tour start at a place that's associated with me."

Lovie could see the pain and bitterness etched on Saxon's face, and it broke her heart.

Her sister, Layla, was going through a similar situation.

She couldn't continue to beg him to host the signing, but she also couldn't afford to breach her contract. She'd practically spent the money already.

"I didn't know any of this when I agreed to promote the book tour... I feel like I've pulled the scab off a gaping wound," she sighed, absently staring at her drink. "What the hell am I gonna do now?"

CHAPTER 3
Saxon

Saxon watched Lovie carefully, noting the conflict playing across her features. He'd only met her a few days ago, but he already knew that she was persistent and determined to fight for what she wanted.

She had come back to his store even after he had treated her so brusquely and had almost literally thrown her out onto the street. Yet here she was, and she had brought gifts.

He cleared his throat. "You said your sister is going through a divorce?" he asked suddenly, changing the subject.

Lovie nodded. "She's out of work as well, thanks to her ex, and staying with me temporarily." She sighed heavily before continuing, her voice full of sadness.

"Her kids were the ones you bought books for?"

"Yeah," she admitted, though Saxon could tell that she wasn't entirely comfortable talking about it. "I'm so happy that my nieces love to read, and you have a good selection in the clearance section," she admitted sheepishly. "I probably spent more than I should have, but I want to encourage their love of learning as much as possible."

Saxon nodded in understanding and approval—he knew how important it was to nurture a child's natural curiosity about the world around them by providing them with books they could read and enjoy. He made a conscious effort to stock children's books from diverse authors so that his customers had plenty of options when they looked for books that featured children that they could identify with.

"You bought that bourbon. I'm sure that set you back a good bit?"

Why was he digging into her finances?

Her expression changed. "Most times when you get a gift, you say thank you and leave it at that."

He held up a hand. "I'm not being ungrateful, I appreciate the gesture, it sounds like," Saxon knew he needed to tread carefully now, "maybe the purchase stretched an already tight budget?"

She placed her mug on the table and then crossed her arms. Saxon could feel the heat from her glare.

Oh hell.

Why did he go there?

"Hey... I'm sorry," he said, backpedaling as fast as he could. "That was out of line. I didn't mean to pry."

"It's fine," she said finally, picking up her mug again. "I read that you worked on Wall Street before moving back to start your bookstore. I'm sure you've never made any questionable financial decisions."

He heard the snark in the last comment, but she wasn't glaring at him any longer. He could live with that.

Saxon gave her a wry smile. "Remember Theranos, the blood testing company that was supposed to revolutionize the healthcare industry?"

Lovie paused, then nodded. "Isn't the woman who founded the company facing criminal charges?"

"Yep. Guess who was an early investor?" he said with a sheepish grin.

"I suppose I know who not to take stock tips from in the future," she said, teasing him. "But seriously, I gave you that bourbon because I thought you'd enjoy it, and yes, I thought it might help persuade you to do the book signing, but I get it."

Saxon sipped his coffee and thought hard for a moment. What could he do to resolve this situation in a way that would be satisfactory to them both? Finally, he made his decision.

"I can't promise anything," he began slowly, looking her in the eye. "But I'll think about it."

"Thank you." Lovie looked up at him, studying him. "Why?"

His eyebrows rose. He hadn't expected the question. "Why will I think about it?"

"Yes. I sure as hell wouldn't do it if the tables were turned. Granted, I've never been married, but I wouldn't do this for any of my exes after they wrote a damning book about our relationship." She folded her arms, waiting for his answer.

Saxon shrugged noncommittally and tried to find the right words to explain his thoughts. "I know how hard it is to get a new business off the ground," he said carefully before deciding against telling her his fear that Sloane was up to something and that Lovie might get caught in the middle if she didn't have someone watching out for her.

Instead, he said simply, "So if there's anything I can do to help you succeed, then I want to try."

Lovie's shoulders relaxed slightly, and he felt some strange urge to protect her. She hadn't asked to be placed in the center of his toxic relationship with his ex-wife, but Saxon was sure this was just the beginning.

Maybe if he agreed to the event and gave Sloane all the publicity she could handle, she'd take the win and move on with her life so that he could move on with his.

Lovie was an innocent bystander in all of this.

Sure, she could have done more digging before agreeing to sign on as Sloane's publicist, but she had no clue how vindictive her new client could be. Sloane, Saxon well knew, was a master at hiding her true nature.

He hadn't known, and he was married to her.

Saxon's thoughts were interrupted by Lovie's voice. "I know this isn't easy for you, so I appreciate that you're considering it."

He shook his head. "It's not about me."

Lovie smiled, and the warmth in her expression made Saxon feel something he couldn't quite put into words. It had been a long time since he had felt that way with anyone. Maybe it was just the coffee, but he found himself wanting to spend more time with her.

He ran a hand over his head, trying to shake off the sudden distraction. "Let me think about it and give you an answer tomorrow. I'll need to talk to my staff and make sure we're all on the same page before we agree to anything."

Lovie nodded. "Of course. Thank you, Saxon."

She finished her cappuccino, and they both stood up to leave. Saxon walked her to the door, and as they crossed the street to head back to the bookstore, he felt a drop of rain hit his forehead. Within seconds, a downpour began, and the street emptied out as people scattered for cover.

Saxon looked at Lovie, who was shivering in her thin sweater. "Come on."

He grabbed her hand and pulled her under the awning of a nearby building. They stood there in silence for a few seconds, watching the rain come down in sheets.

Lovie's hand was still in his, and he could feel her fingers trembling slightly. He wanted to say something to break the tension, but nothing came to mind. He settled for squeezing her hand gently, hoping it would convey the comfort he wanted to offer.

She was staring at their intertwined fingers, and then her gaze rose to meet his.

Their eyes locked, and Saxon felt a jolt of electricity bolt through him. Lovie's eyes filled with something that he couldn't quite decipher. Her lips were parted slightly, and Saxon found himself leaning in closer to her. Before he knew it, their lips were nearly touching. He felt her body relax into his, and all thoughts of the rain surrounding them evaporated.

Saxon's hands were on her waist, pulling her closer to him as he desperately wanted to kiss her. But in that moment, something made him pause, and instead, he pulled back. His eyes searched hers for any sign of understanding or regret. They both remained breathless, yet Saxon couldn't help but feel a sense of longing lingering between them.

Lovie's face was flushed, and her breathing was ragged. Saxon could tell she wanted to kiss him just as badly as he wanted to kiss her.

But there was something holding her back, and he didn't want to push her. Not when they were both vulnerable and emotional from the earlier conversation.

Instead, he smiled at her and said, "I should get you back to your car before you catch a cold."

Lovie nodded, and they both stepped out from under the awning. The rain had lightened up, but it was still coming down steadily. They walked the few blocks in silence, the tension between them palpable.

They reached Lovie's car. Saxon opened the driver's side door for her, breathing in the scent of her, a warm, spicy combo of berries and vanilla that was driving him insane trying to identify the perfume. "I've decided to host her signing. Stop by tomorrow, and we can start working out the details."

She nodded solemnly. "Are you sure?"

He might as well be truthful. "No, but I'm doing it anyway. I'll see you in the morning." He watched her drive off and wondered what he was getting himself into. Closing his eyes, he took a deep breath, trying to push away the memory of the last time he had spoken to Sloane. It was an argument that had ended their marriage and shattered his heart.

He had come home early from work, hoping to surprise Sloane with dinner and a bottle of her favorite wine. But he found her in bed with another man when he walked into their bedroom.

The sight had taken his breath away, and he stood there in shock as Sloane tried to explain it.

"It's not what it looks like," she said, but Saxon had seen enough. He packed his bags and left, unable to even look at her without feeling sick.

The divorce had been messy, with Sloane throwing every insult and accusation she could think of at him. She accused him of neglecting her, of being too focused on his store. She even insinuated that he was the one who cheated.

It had taken months for Saxon to recover from the betrayal and the lies, but he finally moved on with his life.

Despite the hurt and anger he had felt toward Sloane, there was still a part of him that loved her. He spent years with her, building a life together. It was hard to just let go of all that they had shared.

But now, seeing Lovie again had stirred something in him that he hadn't felt in a long time. The way her hand felt in his, the way their eyes locked, it was like a spark had been ignited in him.

He couldn't deny the attraction he felt toward her, but he also knew he had to be careful. He couldn't let his feelings for her cloud his judgment. Sloane was still out there, and he didn't know what she was capable of.

But as he walked back to his store, his mind kept drifting back to Lovie. He couldn't stop thinking about her, about that almost-kiss they had shared. He wanted to see her again, to feel that electricity between them.

Saxon knew he was playing with fire, but he couldn't resist the pull he felt toward Lovie. He just had to be careful not to get burned.

Saxon stepped into the back room of his store, where his intern, Mason, was organizing a stack of books. The young man looked up and grinned when he saw Saxon.

"Hey, Mr. S, I finished the website updates if you want to take a look."

Saxon smiled back. "Good, I appreciate your getting those updates done so quickly."

Mason nodded, his eyes sparkling with enthusiasm. "No problem. I added a new AI chatbot that will answer customer questions based on our FAQs page, which I also updated."

Saxon chuckled. "Glad to hear it. Listen, I wanted to talk to you about something. I've decided to host a book signing for Sloane St. James, and since her book has been trending on BookTok, we'll need to create some content around it."

Mason's expression shifted to one of confusion. "Wait, my mom bought that book. She told me that Sloane St. James is your ex-wife?"

Saxon nodded grimly. He knew news of the signing and Sloane's return to town would fuel the gossip mills for weeks.

Mason hesitated. "Okay."

Saxon raised a brow. Clearly, his intern had concerns.

"What is it, Mason? You can speak freely," Saxon said, taking a seat on one of the nearby chairs.

Mason rubbed the back of his neck. "I just think it might be a bad idea to have a public event with your ex-wife, you know? My mom said it was good that she left and that your ex-wife treated you like sh—"

Saxon eyed the young man.

"Like crap," he finished, looking away.

Saxon nodded thoughtfully. "I understand your concerns, but I've thought it through. Hosting the book signing is not just about Sloane; it's also about promoting the store and getting new customers. Plus, I don't want to let my personal life interfere with business decisions."

Mason looked unconvinced. "If you say so, Mr. S."

Saxon ran a hand over his beard. "Look, I appreciate your honesty, but I've already made up my mind. I need your help in creating content for the signing and promoting it on social media. Can I count on you for that?"

Mason nodded. "Yeah, of course. I'll get right on it."

Saxon could tell Mason wasn't completely on board with the idea, but he appreciated the young man's dedication to the store and his willingness to help out.

"Thanks, Mason. I knew I could count on you."

CHAPTER 4

Lovie

Lovie glanced at her reflection in the mirror again. Was her lipstick too red? Now that Saxon had agreed to the signing, she didn't want to come across as trying to seduce or entice him. She bared her teeth. Yep, there was a trace of the red on her front teeth. Scrubbing at them, she considered the thought. Was she subconsciously trying to entice him?

No, of course not.

Immediately, that near kiss in the rain flashed through her brain. She'd seen the desire in Saxon's eyes and saw him push it back, which relieved and disappointed her in equal measure.

Saxon was an attractive man, she'd admit. Almost too attractive for his own good.

With skin the color of heated toffee and an athlete's tall, muscular body, she'd spent the previous night wide awake, conjuring scenarios where that near kiss was anything but. Where Saxon explored her whole body with that sexy mouth of his.

She shouldn't be thinking such NSFW thoughts about her client's ex-husband.

Ex-husband.

Lovie still couldn't believe Saxon and Sloane had been

married. She had yet to meet Sloane in person, but she'd watched some teaser videos Sloane had done to promote the book.

She wondered about their marriage and glanced at the book in question: *Woman on Top: How to Get Everything You Want From Your Relationships, Your Career and Your Life* by Sloane St. James.

Now that she knew exactly who Sloane was writing about, curiosity had her wanting to read the book again. She grimaced. Maybe not.

The advice Sloane offered leaned heavily into an individualized view of marriage where she insisted that the traditional views of women submitting to men were outdated and women should strive to be the head of the family. According to Sloane, women needed to demand everything they wanted and to be extremely aggressive about it. This approach seemed like a recipe for disaster on all fronts, but to each her own, she sighed.

She didn't want to be the head of the household or the submissive doormat; she wanted a partner in love and life, but that seemed to be too much to ask. Not that she had the time or inclination to date lately.

Lovie shook her head, trying to push away the thoughts of her dismal dating life and Sloane's book. She should focus on the task at hand.

Before entering the store, Lovie stopped to get coffee and bagels for Saxon and the small bookstore staff to grease the wheels of progress. She'd need their help, and her grandmother had drilled into them that you got more flies with honey.

As she walked into the bookstore, Lovie felt a flutter of nerves in her stomach. What if he'd thought about it overnight, decided he didn't want to go there with his ex and canceled?

She pushed the thoughts away, determined to put on a good face no matter what happened. As she approached his office door, she saw Saxon sitting there looking every bit as delicious as she remembered.

His dark hair looked freshly cut, and the long-sleeved, button-down shirt he wore fit him like a glove. How would it feel to run her hands over the fabric, to feel his warm skin beneath it? How would he react?

Stop it, Lovie. You are a professional publicist, not a lonely, sex-starved singleton who hasn't had a good date in months.

Reminding herself that alone and lonely were two distinct things, and she wasn't lonely, she took a deep breath, plastered on a smile, and rapped on his door quickly to announce herself. "Good morning!"

All of Lovie's doubts faded as she watched Saxon's eyes widen in surprise when she placed the cup of coffee from his usual café in front of him. "That's for me?"

"Of course," she said with a triumphant smile, "I was there getting one for myself and figured I'd get you one too."

He nodded, taking a sip. "This is my usual," he said, and the pleasure in his voice made her want to grin stupidly at him.

"Yeah, apparently, you don't stray far from your favorites at any of the local eateries around here. Everyone knows what you like."

He shrugged. "If it ain't broke... you know how the saying goes." He flashed a boyish grin that made her want to cup his face with her hands and kiss him thoroughly.

Lovie cleared her throat, trying to shake off the unprofessional thoughts that were threatening to take over. "So, about the signing," she said, taking a seat across from him.

Saxon leaned back in his chair, his eyes on her. "You live in Charlotte, right?"

She nodded. "Yep, born and raised."

"So, you're going to leave your man behind for a few weeks while you're touring around with Sloane?"

"Any man I'm with needs to be able to fend for himself while I'm away." She raised an eyebrow at him. "But I appreciate your concern."

Saxon chuckled. "I wasn't concerned, just making conversation."

Lovie smiled, feeling her nerves ease slightly. "Well, in that case, I have to ask. Are you planning on coming to any of the signings?"

Saxon shook his head. "No, I don't think so. I don't exactly want to be in the same room with Sloane if I can help it."

A pang of anxiety stabbed her. Why was he going through with this signing? Clearly, there was bad blood between the former couple.

She sighed. As much as she desperately needed this event and the money it would bring, she couldn't let him do this. "Are you really sure you want to host this signing?"

Saxon looked at her intently, his eyes scanning her face. Lovie found herself holding her breath, waiting for his response. Finally, he nodded. "Yeah, I'm sure. It's a business decision, not a personal one."

Lovie nodded. Saxon seemed to be resolute. "Fair enough. Is there anything else you want me to know or any questions you have before we get started?"

Saxon leaned forward, his eyes intense. "Actually, there is one thing I wanted to discuss with you."

Lovie swallowed, feeling a twinge of nerves again. "Okay, what's that?"

Saxon hesitated for a moment before speaking. "Yesterday, when we were in the rain... I just wanted to say that I'm sorry if I crossed a line. I didn't mean to make you uncomfortable or anything."

Lovie's heart skipped a beat, and she felt a rush of heat spreading through her body. "It's fine," she managed to say, trying to keep her voice steady. "I felt fine."

Did she know any other words besides "fine"?

Lovie took another deep breath, willing her heart to slow down as she tried to think of something else to say. But before she could, Saxon spoke again.

"So, do you have any other questions or anything else I should know?"

You should know that since I walked in that door, I can't get you out of my head. That I wanted you to kiss me. Lovie tried to ignore the flutter in her stomach. "Not much. I just wanted to go over a few details with you."

"Shoot."

Lovie forced herself to focus and launched into her plans for the event. Saxon listened attentively, nodding and asking questions when necessary. As they talked, Lovie found herself relaxing, enjoying the easy back and forth between them.

She noticed the way Saxon's eyes lingered on her lips as she spoke, and a rush of heat swept through her. Was it possible he was feeling the same attraction she was?

No, she scolded herself. He was her client's ex-husband, and she needed to keep things strictly professional.

"Okay, so that's the plan for the signing," she said, wrapping up the conversation. "Are you good with everything?"

"Yep, just make sure we get a copy of the tour schedule and the event plan. I'll get the books ordered."

He stood. "Do you have a few minutes?"

Lovie wanted to hug him for agreeing to host the signing, but she controlled herself. "Sure, what's up?"

"I was a less than gracious host the other day and didn't give you a tour of the store. Would you like one now?" He was like a little boy, eager to show off his new train set. Her heart thudded, and she tried to maintain a casual air. "I'd like that."

He nodded and led her from his office into the main floor of the store. He pointed out the bourbon-tasting area. "I rotate about ten different brands here, all from local distilleries, usually around a quarterly theme. Since it's fall, these are all a bit on the sweeter side with notes of spice."

There was an antique glass case with additional bottles of bourbon gracing the shelves. "What are those?" she asked, pointing at the case. "Ultimate top-shelf stuff?"

"Pretty much. Those are my collector's bottles. Not to brag, but there's about twenty thousand dollars worth of bourbon in that case."

She just stared. Who paid that much for throat-burning, fancy moonshine? But she kept her thoughts to herself.

Lovie followed him, trying to focus on the tour and not the way his shirt pulled tightly across his broad shoulders. As they made their way through the store, Saxon showed her the different sections and explained how they were organized.

Lovie tried to pay attention, but she couldn't help stealing glances at him as they walked. She noticed how his muscles moved beneath his button-down shirt as he gestured and how his eyes crinkled at the corners when he smiled.

Stop it, Lovie. You're here to work, not to fantasize about your client's ex.

They stopped in the mystery/thriller section, and he pulled a hardback from the shelf. "You said you like mysteries... have you read this yet?"

She peered at the title. "*Razorblade Tears*... no, I haven't. Is it scary? I don't do scary."

"Not scary. It's good, fast-paced. And we have a few copies signed by the author." He handed the book to her. "My gift to you. Let me know what you think."

She clutched the book to her chest, like he might change his mind and pluck it from her arms.

She couldn't wait to start reading it; she loved a good mystery.

Why had Sloane let this man go? "Thank you, I'll do that."

He led her to a carpeted staircase. "On to the screening room. Watch your step."

As they descended the stairs, Lovie marveled. The bookshop didn't look that big from the outside.

He extended his arm. "This is our media/screening room. We have movie afternoons for kids, book clubs can meet here, and you can rent it out for private showings."

There were two rows of seats, allowing for ten people to sit comfortably in plush leather recliners.

An old-fashioned popcorn maker stood at the ready in the

back corner of the room. "This is such a nice space. Do you ever sit down here and watch movies after the store is closed?"

He shook his head. "No. I built it, hoping Sloane would like it and we'd have date nights down here, but"—he motioned vaguely—"that clearly didn't turn out as I'd planned."

Lovie felt a pang of sympathy for Saxon. She knew what it was like to have life toss a grenade that sent you in a different direction.

"I'm sorry," she said softly. "That must have been hard for you."

Saxon shrugged. "It's okay. I've moved on."

But the way he said it, the hint of sadness in his voice, made Lovie wonder if he really had moved on. She shook her head, trying to push the thought away.

Maybe this signing wasn't a good idea.

She couldn't afford to get involved with him, no matter how attracted she was to him.

"Thanks for the tour," she said, trying to sound casual. "I should probably get going."

Saxon nodded. "Yeah, of course. Let me know if there's anything else you need."

As they walked back up the stairs, Lovie could feel the tension building between them. She tried to keep her eyes focused on the steps in front of her, but she couldn't resist stealing glances at Saxon. He was so handsome, so charming.

Mason, one of the part-time store clerks, was waiting on them when they reached the main level. "Hey, Mr. S, a woman from some winery I can't pronounce just called to confirm you were doing their virtual tasting tonight. I thought you didn't like wine?"

Lovie smirked. Mason sounded a bit offended.

Saxon swore softly. "I forgot about that tasting." He turned to the student. "I don't like most of it, but they talked me into a virtual tasting. They want me to consider carrying their wines in the store."

She stood, incredulous. Lovie loved red wine and was planning to stop at the grocery store on her way back to the hotel for a bottle that she could enjoy while she read the book from Saxon. "You're thinking of carrying wine as well?"

He pursed his lips. "I haven't decided yet, but we might be able to get more of the women in for book club meetings if we offer wine." Saxon turned to the student. "Thanks, Mason. The bottles they sent are in the storage room. Can you bring them out and set up the video conference in the media room?"

They watched the young man hurry off, and Saxon crossed his arms. "Do you like wine?"

"I love wine. More than bourbon, if I'm being honest," she said.

He looked at her, clearly aghast. "Watch your mouth, woman. That's like saying you prefer lima beans over pizza."

She scoffed. "What? Not remotely the same thing."

"We'll debate that later... would you mind sitting in on the wine tasting for the first few minutes? I've got a call I need to take. A woman named Daphne is my rep. Tell her I'll be in shortly," he said, glancing at his watch." It starts in about thirty minutes."

Lovie's heart skipped a beat at the invitation. She knew she should head back to the hotel, but the thought of learning more about wine and tasting wine that was probably new to her was too tempting to resist.

"I'd love to," she said, trying to sound nonchalant.

Saxon looked relieved. "Good, I'll try to wrap the call up as fast as I can. Oh, if you want to eat something beforehand, I have an account at the Italian restaurant down the street, Rosa's Italian Kitchen. They deliver, so just call and give them my name."

Lovie nodded, trying to focus on the conversation and not the sensual way Saxon's lips moved when he was giving orders.

He stopped at his office door as he filled her in on the details of the virtual tasting. "It's with a relatively new French winery. They sent me the bottles and included some cheeses as well."

Lovie closed the door behind her and made her way back down

to the media room. She surveyed the room. Definitely a man's touch. The room was tastefully done but full of dark wood, bulky recliners, and large movie posters. It screamed Saxon, and she found herself smiling at the image of him deliberating over fabric swatches.

Stretched out in one of the recliners in front of the huge projection screen, she found the Italian restaurant's website, scanned the menu, and realized she had no idea what Saxon might want to eat. Lovie wanted a salad so she'd have plenty of room for the wine. She drummed her fingers on the recliner, then dialed the number. "Hi, I'm calling from The Book Barrel. We want to place an order for delivery."

"Of course." Then, a pause. "This isn't Sloane." The statement wasn't a question.

Lovie frowned. "No, this is Lovie?" Why was she asking like she didn't know her own name?

"Oh, ok, yes of course," Lovie heard the woman chuckle with what sounded like relief. "Let me guess...the usual for Saxon? I put aside the last of the spaghetti and meatballs for him, yes?"

"That's perfect, thanks, and a Caesar salad with chicken."

"Got it. Your name is Lovie?" She could hear the woman's curiosity.

"That's me. Are you Rosa?"

The woman clucked. "No, she was my mother. I'm Delfina. You are a new employee or new lady friend?"

How was she supposed to answer that?

"New publicist."

"Ah. Ok, Lovie, you should come in for lunch one day when you want a good hearty meal. Ask for Delfina. Tell Saxon we'll get this order over in about twenty minutes."

Lovie checked her watch. The food would probably arrive right when the tasting started. Oh well, maybe she'd stick the salad in the refrigerator and eat it afterward.

Hands on her hips, she surveyed the space. The recliners were nice, but she had an idea.

There was a large upholstered bench against the back wall, and she cautiously pushed on it to see if it would open. It gave, and she peered in.

A handful of colorful throws were folded neatly inside, and she picked out what she hoped was the largest one.

Lovie shook it open. The throw was plush and perfect for snuggling on a chilly fall night. She hurried back over to the open area between the screen and the first row of recliners and spread the throw out like they were having a picnic. The fit was perfect, and she took the tray that held the wine bottles and glasses, placing it in the center of the throw. She found napkins and placed them on the tray. She was all set. She just needed Saxon to join her.

When it was time for the virtual tasting, the French winemaker appeared on the screen, speaking in heavily accented English about the wines they were about to taste.

"You're not Saxon, I assume?" Daphne Milliard asked, raising an eyebrow as she peered at Lovie through the screen.

"No, I'm Lovie. He's wrapping up a call and asked me to get us started."

Daphne nodded. "Lovely name. Well, he'll just have to catch up. We'll start with the full-bodied wines and finish with the lighter options. This first full-bodied wine has notes of spice, ripe fruit, and soft tannins. Please, pour yourself a glass, and let's toast to a wonderful evening."

Saxon was still upstairs, and Lovie debated on whether she should pour his glass. She shrugged. Might as well. She poured the deep red wine into his glass, then into her own.

Lovie swirled it around, taking in the aroma before taking a sip. It was a deep, fragrant red, and she closed her eyes, emitting a soft moan as she savored the wine.

"If it elicits that kind of response from all my customers, maybe I should start selling wine," Saxon's deep voice behind her made her jump slightly.

"It's amazing," she said, opening her eyes. "I can taste the spice and a hint of oak. It's so smooth."

Daphne continued, describing the wine they tasted, a full-bodied Bordeaux, and she chatted with the winemaker about the grapes and the aging process.

The winemaker gave them a five-minute break to cue up the next wine and told them she'd be right back with the next bottle.

She watched nervously as Saxon took in her makeshift picnic. Now that she took everything in, the setting was kind of romantic, like they were on a date. She hadn't meant to convey anything like that.

"This is nice. I would have never thought to set the room up like this." He motioned to the throw. "Can I join you or are you waiting for someone?" he joked.

"That's your glass and your spaghetti and meatballs. Try the wine, it's amazing."

"So I heard." He smirked at her over his glass.

He sipped. "That is actually pretty good."

Saxon turned to Lovie, his eyes wide. "How'd you learn so much about wine?"

Lovie laughed, feeling a little embarrassed. "I've just always been interested in it. I've taken a few classes and visited a few wineries. Plus, I love a good Bordeaux."

Saxon smiled. "Well, you definitely know more than I do. I just know what I like and what I don't like."

They continued with the tasting, trying different wines and cheeses.

Daphne shared stories about her family, winemakers for generations, and how she'd grown up surrounded by grapevines.

After the last bottle from the kit was sampled, Daphne concluded the tasting and wished them both a good evening. Lovie and Saxon continued to sip and chat as the night wore on. Their conversation evolved from wine and bourbon to travel. Lovie listened with rapt attention as Saxon told her about his most recent trip to Ghana and Cape Verde in Africa.

Saxon asked Lovie about her life in Charlotte, and she shared funny stories about her precocious nieces and her plans for her public relations business. She felt oddly comfortable sharing her ideas with him, even though her sister had deemed most of them unrealistic.

Before Lovie knew it, it was late, and they were both a little tipsy. A warmth she couldn't fully attribute to the wine filled her chest as she realized she was having fun with Saxon.

She was captivated, and she knew she should leave. She tried to push the attraction away, reminding herself that this was her client's ex and that she shouldn't complicate things, but she was having a good time.

"I should probably go," she said, trying to stand up and failing miserably. Saxon caught her before she fell and held her close.

"You okay?"

Lovie blinked. Saxon appeared to have two sets of eyes and two noses. She giggled. "I might be a touch tipsy."

Saxon chuckled. "Maybe we should have had more food."

Lovie smiled, enjoying the feel of his arms around her. "Maybe."

They stood there for a moment, swaying slightly. Saxon's breath on her neck was sending little sparks racing through her body. He could kiss her there, and she'd dissolve. She needed to distract herself from those thoughts. She turned to face him.

Their eyes met, and at that moment, all her reservations disappeared. Lovie leaned in, pressing her lips to Saxon's. At first, he seemed surprised, but then he responded eagerly, deepening the kiss.

It was as if a floodgate had been opened, and all the pent-up desire they had been feeling for each other was unleashed. They broke apart briefly, panting for breath, and then Saxon was kissing her again, his hands roaming over her body.

Lovie moaned, her body responding to his touch. She knew she should pull away, that this was a bad idea, but she couldn't bring herself to do it. She was too caught up in the moment.

Lovie pulled away. "I should be getting back to my room."

He shook his head. "Neither of us is fit to be behind the wheel." He ran a hand over the small of her back. "So, you can either call a ride share or, hang out with me tonight."

She cocked her head at him. "Is this how you normally seduce women? Ply them with wine and then take them upstairs?"

"Nope, it's normally bourbon." He grinned at her, and Lovie's insides did that melting thing again.

"Actually, I figured if I couldn't get my wife to join me down here for a date, why would any other woman be interested?"

"Well, for what it's worth, I know this wasn't a date, but I enjoyed myself, so thanks for inviting me."

Saxon smiled, his eyes lingering on her lips. "I enjoyed myself too, and as for the not-a-date, well, I think we both know that's not entirely true anymore."

Lovie's heart thumped in her chest. She knew she was treading on dangerous ground, but the pull between them was too strong to resist.

"So, what do you say?" he asked, his voice husky. "Want to stay and keep me company?"

CHAPTER 5

Saxon

"I don't think that's a good idea," she said softly, breaking the spell between them. "I'm not ready for that tonight."

Saxon sighed and stepped back, his face serious and intense. "I understand." He ran a hand down her arm, his gaze still lingering on hers. "How about I put you up in my guest room? That way, you can get some rest without having to worry about driving back to your hotel tonight."

Saxon watched her, an inner debate visible on her face. He squeezed her hand. "I'd take you back to your hotel if I could but I promise to be on my best behavior tonight. Scout's honor."

"You were a Boy Scout?"

"Nah, I never liked the uniforms."

She rolled her eyes. "Why doesn't that surprise me? You were probably one of those kids who always wore the latest trends."

He shook his head. "Nah. My aunt and uncle took me in after my parents died and they were about function over fashion."

Lovie turned to fully face him. "Part of me wants to go upstairs to your room with you, but we shouldn't, right?"

Saxon ran a thumb over her jaw. He had that same battle going on within him. "Probably not." He kissed her forehead. "When's the last time you binge watched a show?"

"Umm...never? I have too much to do." Lovie eyed him.

"You game for watching Abbott Elementary with me for a little while? I might have an opportunity to get the cast into the store for an event," he said. He wasn't ready to part ways for the evening.

"Maybe," Pointing at the popcorn maker, she asked, "is that an option?"

Saxon grinned, his heart lifting at her response. "Popcorn it is." He led her towards the media room, his hand on her lower back, feeling the warmth of her body through her dress. He could sense her hesitation, and he wanted to reassure her that he wasn't expecting anything from her tonight.

As they settled onto the throw, Saxon fished out the remote from between the cushions and turned on the television. He scrolled through the streaming options before settling on Abbott Elementary.

Lovie snuggled into his side, her head on his shoulder. Saxon wrapped an arm around her, his hand resting on her hip. He could feel the softness of her curves against him, and it was taking every ounce of his willpower not to give into temptation.

As they watched the show, Saxon found himself getting lost in the plot and the characters. He was impressed with the writing and the performances, and he knew that this could be a great opportunity for his store. But despite his focus on the show, he couldn't ignore the warmth of Lovie's body pressed against him, and the feel of her heartbeat.

He turned his head slightly, catching a whiff of her perfume. It was intoxicating, and he found himself wanting to bury his face in her hair and breathe her in.

As if reading his thoughts, Lovie shifted closer to him, her hand coming to rest on his chest. Saxon's heart thundered in his chest.

She was so close.

But taking her to bed wasn't protecting her from Sloane. He

needed to remember that. Sloane wasn't going to take the news that her publicist was sleeping with her ex-husband well.

He glanced down at Lovie as she dozed, her head on his shoulder. He should wake her and put her to bed. In the guest bedroom.

Saxon let himself imagine carrying her to his room, stripping off the curve hugging knit dress she wore and letting her strip him. He exhaled sharply. He didn't need those thoughts right now.

Gently, Saxon shook Lovie awake. "Hey, it's getting late. Let me show you to the guest bedroom."

Lovie blinked, looking around the room as if she had forgotten where she was. "Oh, right. Sorry, I must have dozed off."

Saxon stood up and offered her his hand, helping her to her feet. He led her upstairs to the top level where his living quarters were, then down a short hallway to a door at the end of the hall, opening it to reveal a spacious guest bedroom.

Lovie stepped inside, looking around the room. "Wow, this is beautiful," she said, turning to face Saxon. "Thank you for letting me stay here tonight."

"Anytime...did you want a t-shirt or something to sleep in?" He hoped she wouldn't say that she slept nude or anything. He couldn't handle that.

Lovie nodded. "Yes, that would be great."

She was standing there in the room, way too close to the bed, looking like she wanted him like he wanted her.

He cleared his throat, broke his gaze, and hurried out of the room.

In his own room, Saxon pulled a clean Book Barrel t-shirt, one of the first he'd had designed when the store opened, and held it up. It was going to be big on her but it should work.

He walked back to the guest room and knocked on the door. Lovie opened it, looking a little surprised to see him again so soon.

"Here you go," he said, handing her the t-shirt. "You can keep it. I have tons of those. I overordered when I first opened." He shrugged, realizing he was babbling.

"Thanks," she said, taking the shirt from him. "I'll take some pics in it for my social media while I'm in town."

"I appreciate that," And he did. He wasn't used to anyone besides his family caring enough to promote his store. Sloane had never liked the idea of his running a bookstore. She thought it beneath him.

Lovie wasn't Sloane. He needed to remember that. Sloane would never have sat on a throw and asked him questions about his store and his love of literature.

He shook his head, clearing the memories of his marriage. "My room is one door down if you need anything. See you in the morning."

He turned, afraid that if he stayed, he'd have her on her back moaning his name before either of them knew what happened.

He needed a cold, cold shower.

The next morning when Saxon tapped on her door, Lovie didn't answer. He knocked again then pushed the door open.

She was gone.

Saxon let out a sigh as he leaned against the doorframe. He had hoped to see her before she left, but it seemed that she had left early. He couldn't blame her, after all, she had a busy schedule. But he couldn't help feeling a little disappointed.

Walking back to his room, he took a quick shower before heading down to the store.

Saxon turned on the lights and made sure everything was functioning properly.

He had a routine he followed each morning before the store opened for the day. First, he made sure all the books were in their proper place on the shelves. He straightened any crooked piles, dusted off the covers of the new arrivals, and made sure the display tables were properly arranged to showcase the latest titles.

He checked his emails and processed the online orders that had come in after the store closed. He'd have Mason pull the books and get them packaged when he came in later that morning.

Saxon was on his second cup of coffee and fully engrossed in restocking shelves with a famous local author's cookbooks when the door chime sounded and a female voice called out his name.

He stood up and headed to the front.

He looked up and saw his cousins Gia, Noemie, and Jordyn walking towards him. Gia was his Uncle Charlie's daughter and Noemie was married to Gia's brother, Jameson. Jordyn was technically his cousin once removed but who was saying all of that?

"Ah hell, what brings the terror squad in on a Saturday morning?" He chuckled.

"Good morning to you too, Sunshine," Gia said, a huge smile on her face. "We have some news!"

Saxon crossed his arms, giving them his full attention. "What's going on?"

"I'm engaged!" Gia held up her hand, showing off the ring on her finger.

Saxon took his cousin's hand, examining the sparkling diamond. "Wow, G... this is the real thing. Your man did a good job."

"Of course he did. Isn't it beautiful?" She wiggled her fingers as the ring sparkled, reflecting the light.

He grabbed her in a bear hug. "Congrats, G... when's the wedding?"

"I'm not sure yet. We've had a Christmas wedding in the family, I'm thinking New Year's Eve, then we can all have a big party to celebrate our anniversaries and Noemie's birthday," she looked at Noemie. "That might be fun, right? A New Year's Eve wedding?"

Noemie nodded enthusiastically. "Yes! What better way to ring in the New Year?

Saxon grunted. "You all do realize Christmas is a thing, right? So, we exchange Christmas gifts then we turn around and we gotta buy a wedding gift? There are other holidays throughout the year, you know?"

"Yeah, I know...I guess I could do a spring wedding. But that seems so cliché. Anyway, I want you to be in the wedding as a groomsman."

He winced. That meant he'd need a date. An image of Lovie crossed his vision and he pushed it away. That was a big ask of someone you barely knew, depending on when Gia was holding her event.

But then again, he couldn't ignore the way he felt about Lovie. "Of course, G. I'll be there for you."

She rubbed her hands together. "Good, this is going to be amazing!" Gia swept a hand over the store. "Where are the wedding books? Noemie and Jordyn said they need inspiration," Gia said, picking up a coffee table book on Coco Chanel. "Oh, I haven't seen this before, I might want this one, too."

Saxon nodded, taking the book from her so he could place it at the register. "You know you came to the right place. You all want any bourbon while you search?"

"Not yet, it's still early in the day." Gia and Noemie descended on the wedding planner book aisle, pulling books and stacking them on a display table.

Jordyn hung back and Saxon placed an arm around her shoulders. "What's up, Ms. Jordyn? This is your last year of school, right?"

She heaved a sigh. "Maybe. I want to do event marketing and planning now. But if I switch majors, that's probably another full year of school."

"You can just finish up and take some event planner courses or get an internship with an event venue. Then you have the degree to fall back on. But I say you go ahead and finish when you're supposed to."

She nodded. "That's what my dad said too but I figured he didn't want to pay for an additional year."

He waved her off. "You know your dad will do pretty much whatever you want. That man is the definition of a girl dad."

The bell chimed again and Mason, backpack slung over his shoulders, strode into the store.

Saxon watched him do a double take when he saw Jordyn. His eyes narrowed. "Mason," he motioned the young man over, "this is my little cousin, Jordyn. She's at UK. Jordyn, this is Mason, he's a senior at the University of Louisville. He handles a lot of the tech in the store."

Jordyn slid from under his arm and shook Mason's hand.

"Nice to meet you, Mason," Jordyn said with a shy smile.

"Likewise," Mason replied, his gaze lingering on her a little longer than Saxon deemed necessary. "What brings you in today?"

"We're here for wedding books. My Aunt Gia is getting married," Jordyn said, playing with the hem of her sweater. "I'm a math major, what about you?"

"That's cool...beautiful and smart," Mason said, nodding. "I'm studying computer science and engineering. But I also help Mr. S out with the bookstore."

"Thank you," Jordyn said, biting her lip.

Saxon sighed. He'd make sure his young protegee knew that he would break body parts if Mason hurt Jordyn.

Saxon interrupted their conversation. "All right, lovebirds. No need to get too comfortable in my store," he winked at Jordyn, who looked like she wanted to curl up into a ball and disappear. "Mason, there are some online orders that need to be filled, but why don't you show Jordyn the new sci-fi section first?"

"Yes, sir." The man stood up straighter and led Jordyn to the other side of the store.

"Are you matchmaking, Cousin?" Gia spoke behind him, causing him to jump slightly.

He shrugged, embarrassed to be caught. "Mason's a good kid. Plus, I'll remind him that he doesn't want any Mitchell hands on him if he hurts her."

She rolled her eyes. "You're as bad as Jameson."

"Damn right."

"Anyway, I thought you wanted nothing to do with the opposite sex? Now you're connecting single people?" They watched as Mason pulled books for Jordyn.

"Aww...geek love is the best love," Gia said, placing her chin on her fist.

"Just because I'm a bitter old man doesn't mean other people should suffer."

Gia scoffed. "Please, what are you, forty? That's hardly old. And just because Sloane was the devil's daughter doesn't mean you should give up. And speaking of, you'll need a date for my wedding...what about my friend, Erika?"

He grimaced. He'd met Erika and she was a little too adventurous for his taste. "Ah, I'm good. I'll find someone."

"Yeah, well, just don't break down and bring Sloane, cause I could see her making a move on my groom and I'd hate to punch her out on my day."

He ran a hand over his beard. Gia's assessment wasn't wrong. "I'm not bringing Sloane. That's over." He eyed his petite cousin. "And since when are you throwing punches? When we were kids, you'd just sic me and Jay on your enemies."

"I'm taking kickboxing now...I'll take Sloane down if you need me to." She balled small fists at him and he laughed out loud at the image. "Ok then, Jackie Chan." He looked at his watch. "Look, I have a store to run. Mason will check you out when you're done; let me know when you decide on a date for the wedding, G."

～

After Saxon closed the store for the night and settled into his apartment for the evening, he held his phone in his hand, debating on calling Lovie.

He'd enjoyed his evening with her and wanted to see her again.

But after Sloane, he wasn't sure if he was ready for a relationship. He remembered the way Sloane made him feel, so vulnerable and exposed, and he didn't want to go through that again.

He tapped the phone lightly on his leg, debating. Lovie was different. He felt comfortable around her, like he could be himself without fear of judgment.

He smiled at the thought of her, the way she lit up when she talked about her family and her deep wine knowledge. She had a passion for life he envied. Since his divorce, the only thing that fired him up was his bookstore, but there was more to life than work even if that work was his passion.

Exhaling a deep breath, he dialed her number.

CHAPTER 6

Lovie

Lovie stared at her phone on the nightstand, vibrating as it lit up, indicating she had a call coming in. Her heart beat painfully fast. She knew who it was. She shouldn't answer the phone but she wanted to hear his voice.

Lovie ignored the call, turning the phone over where she couldn't see the display.

Back at home in Charlotte, she took stock of her day.

Once she'd left Saxon's apartment in the wee hours of the morning to avoid the walk of shame past his staff, she'd returned to her hotel to put together a plan of action for Sloane's book tour.

She originally planned to spend the day working and maybe see if Saxon was available to give her a tour of Kissing Springs. After being thoroughly kissed by one of its residents, she loved the name and wanted to see why it was called the Romance Capital of the South.

But after the call she'd gotten earlier, she couldn't let things go any further. She needed to put the brakes on anything between them so she packed up and drove back to her hometown.

The phone stopped ringing and a few seconds later there was a ping, indicating she had a new voice mail message.

She closed her eyes.

Her mind played their kiss on a loop, letting her relive the feel of his lips on hers over and over.

But It wasn't enough. She wanted the real thing.

Lovie picked up the phone and tapped the button to access her messages.

"Hey Lovie, just calling to make sure you got back to the hotel ok. Um, call me or text me and let me know. It's Saxon. Ok. Bye."

She banged her head against the headboard, staring up at the ceiling.

What should she do now?

Maybe ask an expert.

Climbing out of bed, Lovie crept out of her room quietly, she knew her sister had just put the girls to bed, and tapped softly on the guest room door where her older sister was.

"What's up?" her sister asked softly, opening the door with a curious look on her face.

Lovie gestured for her sister to come out into the hallway. "Can I talk to you for a sec?"

"Sure, what's going on?" Layla asked, following her into the living room.

Lovie sat down on the couch, tucking her legs under her and her sister sat down next to her.

"I told you Saxon agreed to host the book signing for Sloane St. James?" Layla nodded and Lovie continued. "Well, I've been dealing with her publisher this whole time and I called them this morning to let them know we're good to go."

Layla nodded again, stifling a yawn. "Sorry, your nieces attempted to wear me all the way out today. Go on."

"Yeah, same. Anyway, Sloane called me to tell me she's excited to work with me, she's heard good things, etc."

"You said she's the bookstore owner's ex-wife?" Layla broke in.

Lovie nodded. "Yep. Apparently, it wasn't an amicable parting of ways. He didn't go into detail but there are references in her book about it."

"She put their dirty laundry in her book?" Layla kissed her teeth. "I wish Kent would..."

Lovie knew she needed to distract her sister before her advice session turned into another of Layla's rants about her ex-husband. "She did, but get this..."

Lovie paused to make sure Layla was paying attention. "She confided in me that she regrets letting Saxon get away."

Layla's head snapped up. "Wait...she put their business in the streets and now she wants him back? I saw her book recommended in Essence Magazine the other day. It's going to blow up if it hasn't already."

"Right. I'm pretty sure Saxon doesn't know that's why she wants to do the signing at his store. Do I warn him?"

And what did she do with her growing attraction to him?

Layla touched her arm, bringing her out of her thoughts. "I get the sense that you like him? Did you two...you know?"

Lovie shook her head. "No, I kissed him and he kissed me back...God, those lips," she put a hand to her mouth, recalling Saxon's lips on hers. "If every man in Kissing Springs can do what Saxon did, I see why the town got its name, anyway, we didn't do anything. We were both kinda drunk...I did a virtual wine tasting, by the way, we need to do that one weekend."

"Wow, well maybe we should all move there. I, of course, will not be kissing anyone ever again cause men suck, but maybe a change of scenery would be good for all of us. It's not like I have a job to go to or a house keeping me here in Charlotte." The last part ended in a bitter laugh.

Lovie chuckled. "Maybe we should. But going back to the issue at hand, what do I do? Should I tell Saxon what Sloane said?"

Layla leaned back against the couch and thought for a moment. "Honestly, I don't know. You barely know this man, and telling him that his ex-wife regrets their divorce might not be the best idea. There's always a chance that they reconcile then you look like the bad guy."

Lovie nodded, considering her sister's advice. "Yeah, you're right." Her shoulders slumped. She always hated to see when marriages failed and maybe they were meant to be together. She didn't want to stand in the way of Saxon's happiness.

But part of her already missed him.

"And as for your growing attraction to him, just be careful. You don't want to get too involved with someone who has a complicated past like that."

Lovie nodded, taking in her sister's advice. "Thanks, Lay. You always know what to say."

Layla grinned. "That's what big sisters are for. Now, tell me more about the virtual wine tasting? And the Bordeaux? And that kiss?"

Lovie smiled, grateful for her sister's distraction tactics. She launched into a description of the virtual wine tasting and the different types of wine they had tried. But as she talked, her mind wandered back to Saxon and the kiss they had shared. She wondered what he was doing right now, if he was thinking about her too.

Layla snapped her fingers and Lovie blinked. "You're thinking about him, aren't you?"

Lovie blushed. "Maybe...just a little."

"Well, I won't judge you. He does sound like a catch. But just be careful, okay? Especially if his ex is still in the picture. Don't mess around and get your heart broken."

Lovie nodded, knowing her sister was right. As much as she liked Saxon, she needed to pull back and put her job first.

They chatted a few minutes more before Layla decided to call it a night. Lovie retreated to her room and picked up her phone.

She closed her eyes, resisting the urge to call him. Instead she typed out a text.

> I'm back in Charlotte. Thank you for everything and I'll be in touch about the signing.

~

Lovie sat in her kitchen at the table, trying and failing to focus on her work. She could see the bright light blue sky from a bay window in the living room. Normally she'd be in her home office, but she'd sacrificed the room when Layla and the girls moved in.

Layla had just gone through a tough divorce and now they'd seen that Layla's ex, Kent, was getting married. Layla had shrieked that the ink on the divorce papers hadn't dried; the lawyers bills hadn't been paid yet and he was tying the knot?

Maybe they did need to move out of North Carolina. Kent hadn't talked to his kids since he'd dropped the bombshell on Layla that he wanted out. And rumor was, he was moving to Florida.

She was looking at her house value on one of the real estate sites and tapped a pen against her lips. The house was worth more than she thought.

Her phone rang and a shiver of anticipation raced through her.

She glanced at the screen. It wasn't Saxon.

It was an unknown number from out of state. Lovie hesitated for a moment before answering. "Hello, Lovie Whitfield PR."

"Hi, is this Lovie?"

"Yes, it is. Who's this?"

"This is Stan Davis. I got your number from Saxon. He said you might be able to help me. I just fired my social media manager and I have a golf course opening in less than a month. I need a whole campaign immediately."

Lovie's heart sank a little at the mention of Saxon's name. "May I ask why you fired that person?"

Stan sighed heavily into the phone. "I just found out the son-of-a-bitch was stealing money and harassing my staff. If you can help me, I'll pay you double your normal rate."

After arranging to meet Stan in his office to review the current campaigns the next day, Lovie prepared a contract for him to sign and packed a bag for her trip back to Kissing Springs.

She decided to take a break from work.

She grabbed her phone and opened her messages, scrolling through until she found Saxon's name. She typed out a message, hesitating before hitting send.

> Hey, thanks for the referral. Just booked
> Stan Davis as a client.

She watched the bubbles indicating he was typing a response.

> Happy to help...you can take me to
> dinner to show your gratitude.

Lovie couldn't help the smile that crossed her lips as she read Saxon's text. Taking him to dinner would just make things worse, put her in deeper danger of falling for him and that wasn't the plan. She had a job to do and that was to create an amazing campaign for Stan Davis—not fall in love with a man who might be getting back with his ex-wife. No, if there were any dinners it would be strictly business only.

She arrived in Kissing Springs later that night and checked into the same hotel she'd used the previous visit. After grabbing a few hours of sleep, Lovie awoke early with a renewed sense of focus and determination.

She showered and dressed in a red silk blouse, black pencil skirt and her favorite black stilettos. As she slid them on, she smirked, recalling Saxon's 'CFM' comment.

Maybe she'd wear them for him again one day. Maybe he'd take her up on her offer.

Lovie arrived at Stan's office, ready to impress him with her ideas for his golf course opening. She had done her research and had a clear understanding of the company's values and goals.

Lovie was shown into his office by his assistant, a young woman with a friendly smile. Stan was a tall, broad-shouldered man with salt-and-pepper hair and piercing blue eyes. He greeted

Lovie with a firm handshake and a smile that didn't quite reach his eyes.

"Thank you so much for coming, Lovie. Sorry for the short notice."

As she presented her ideas, Stan nodded in agreement, occasionally interjecting his own thoughts and suggestions.

At one point, Stan stood up, rolled his neck and focused his eyes on her. "I think we've made good progress. You up for a bite to eat? There's a place near here that serves a mean brisket sandwich."

Wasn't it early for lunch? She glanced at her watch. They'd worked well past noon. Food would be good but barbeque and silk didn't go together. She'd have to be careful and ribs were out of the question. "Sure, let me grab my purse."

At the restaurant, they sat across from each other at a small table. Stan ordered the brisket and Lovie opted for a BBQ chicken salad. As they ate, they continued to discuss the campaign and Lovie found herself impressed by Stan's strategic plans for the new venture.

"Saxon spoke very highly of you. We go back to his Wall Street days and when I mentioned I needed to find someone to replace my social media person, he recommended your company. Are you out of Louisville?"

"No, currently I live in Charlotte," she replied. "And I appreciate his referral. I'm excited about this project."

They were polishing off banana pudding out of Mason jars when Saxon strode over to their table.

"Stan," Saxon said, eyeing Lovie, "I thought the wife banned you from this place after the heart surgery." He clapped the older man on the back.

He turned to Lovie, his brown eyes unreadable. "I didn't know you were back in town, Lovie."

Why did she feel like she'd just been caught with her shirt up over her head in the back of a Buick with the town bad boy?

Lovie took a deep breath, trying to keep her composure as she met Saxon's gaze. "Yes, I'm back in town for business," she said, hoping her voice didn't betray her nerves.

Saxon's lips quirked up into a smirk as he leaned against the table. "Ah, business. Of course." He looked over at Stan. "You're lucky to have her on your team. Lovie's the best."

Stan nodded, clearly impressed. "I can see that already. We've been having a great meeting."

Saxon nodded. "Good, I'll leave you both to it and grab my food. Good seeing you, Stan. Lovie, I'll be in touch."

And with that he turned and walked away.

Lovie watched Saxon go, her heart pounding in her chest. She was relieved when Stan broke the silence.

"Good to see Saxon excited about something other than his store."

Lovie frowned, thinking she'd missed something Stan said. "Oh really?"

"Yep. I'd say you've sparked his interest. I won't pry but he's a good man and he's right, you know," Stan said with a knowing smile. "If you ever decided to relocate to Kissing Springs, there's plenty of new businesses here that could use your services. Give it some thought."

CHAPTER 7

Saxon

S axon collected his to go order and made his way back to his vehicle, thinking about Lovie. Stan was a good guy but he was still a man, and he saw the appreciative looks Stan tossed at Lovie.

A part of Saxon was glad Lovie had come back into town, but a larger part was filled with questions.

Why hadn't she told him she was heading back to town?

For that matter, why had she abruptly left town in the first place?

Maybe she regretted crossing that line with him.

Saxon shook his head. All of these thoughts raced through Saxon's mind as he drove back to his store, all the while trying to quell the jealousy rising in his chest. If anything, he was the one struggling to keep his distance from Lovie.

She was a distraction, one in which he couldn't afford to indulge.

He had a business to run and she lived in Charlotte.

Saxon carried his food back to his office and dug in as he reviewed the event calendar for the coming months.

His thoughts drifted back to Lovie. Damn, he couldn't deny the way he felt when he looked at her. She nailed the

58

professional sexy look in that red silk blouse and slim black skirt.

But he couldn't let himself get carried away with his feelings. He had been burned before, and he didn't want to repeat the mistakes of his past.

Saxon pushed aside thoughts of Lovie and the confusing feelings she stirred up in him. He had a business to run and customers to help.

With that thought in mind, he left his office and strode around his store, greeting each customer with a warm smile and offering assistance.

This was the part of owning a bookstore that he loved: making recommendations and hearing about what people loved to read.

The store kept him busy the rest of the afternoon. He was helping a customer select a bourbon for an upcoming dinner party when Mason, his backpack hitched on his shoulder, waved, indicating he was leaving for the evening. Saxon saluted him and checked the time. The store was supposed to close in minutes.

As Saxon watched the last customer pull out of the parking lot, his phone buzzed.

It was a message from Lovie. Saxon's heart skipped a beat as he swiped the screen to read the text.

> Are you by any chance free for dinner tonight? My treat, as you requested.

He chuckled then typed a reply.

> I might be. Depends on where we're eating.

The response came back quickly.

> What's your favorite restaurant in town?

Saxon felt his heart race at the thought of seeing her again. He took a deep breath and tried to calm himself down.

> The BBQ place where I caught you and
> Stan earlier. But there's a new Mexican
> cantina we can try. I'll pick you up at
> seven?

> Sounds good. I'm at the Hampton Inn.

He arrived at Lovie's hotel at seven to find her waiting outside the hotel. She was wearing a leather bomber and dark bootcut jeans that made her legs look a mile long.

"Hey," she said, beaming at him as he got out to open her door for her.

"Hey," he replied, struggling to keep his voice steady. His nervousness annoyed him and Saxon willed himself to calm down. This was just dinner.

Once they were on the road, Lovie turned to him. "You strike me as a man who likes a five-star steakhouse. Is this one of those gourmet Mexican fusion places that's going to set me back a month?"

He gave her a sidelong glance. "No, this place is very casual from what my cousins say. I wouldn't do that to you. If we go to a five-star steakhouse, it will be my treat."

She paused like she had something on her mind. "Have you dated much since your divorce?" she asked finally.

Saxon's heart skipped a beat at Lovie's question. He wasn't used to being so directly asked about his personal life. "Not really," he admitted after a moment. "I've kind of thrown myself into making the store a success which doesn't leave time for anything serious."

Lovie nodded. "I can relate. I haven't really met anyone who is worth my time lately. It's just easier to be at home curled up with a good book."

Saxon held the door to the restaurant open for her. "As a bookstore owner, that's exactly what I want to hear, but as a man, I wonder about the other fools you've been meeting. What's one thing that makes a man worth your time?"

She was ready with an answer. "Good conversation. I've been on so many dates where I'm sitting there listening to my date drone on and on about himself, like I'm interviewing him."

The Mexican cantina turned out to be a cozy, dimly-lit spot with colorful decor and a bustling bar. Saxon ordered a round of margaritas and some chips and guacamole to start. As they sipped their drinks and dug into the basket of chips, Saxon found himself relaxing into the conversation with Lovie.

"So would it be accurate to say you're finding books more interesting than dating?"

Lovie winced. "When you put it like that...speaking of books, I'm loving Razorblade Tears so far. Thank you again."

"I'm glad you're enjoying it. I got caught up in the story and was up till three in the morning reading. I just couldn't put it down."

Lovie's warm laugh was infectious. "Luckily you're the boss and won't get fired for being late."

He leaned in and lowered his voice. "That next day around lunch time, I told Mason I wasn't to be disturbed and I shut myself in my office for a good nap."

She grinned at him. "I don't think I would have picked it up had you not suggested it. But I love being surprised by a good book. There's something magical about getting lost in a story, isn't there?"

Saxon felt a jolt of electricity run through him as he met her gaze. He couldn't deny the attraction he felt towards her, but at the same time, he knew he needed to tread carefully.

As they perused the menu, Saxon found himself stealing glances at Lovie. She had her hair pulled back into a low ponytail with soft tendrils on either side of her face. He longed to brush one aside and run a hand over the soft planes of her neck and shoulders. He was drawn to her like a moth to a flame, and he knew he shouldn't be.

But there was something about her that he couldn't resist.

The rest of dinner passed in a blur of laughter and easy

conversation. They talked about their favorite books, movies and tv shows growing up.

When the check came, Lovie reached for it. "I've got this," she said firmly.

"You know I was kidding about you owing me dinner. I'm happy that Stan hired you." He reached into his pocket for his wallet.

"No, I asked you out so I'm paying. Stan gave me a very nice retainer and..." she slapped a card down before he could get cash out, "...my sister and I are champion level speed players."

"Speed? As in the card game?" She didn't strike him as a card shark.

"Yep!" Their server scooped up the card and bill then disappeared.

He eyed her. He knew she probably couldn't afford to treat him to dinner and she'd never admit it.

Saxon stood up. "Did you see where the bathrooms were?"

Lovie shook her head.

Saxon rubbed his hands together. Perfect. "I'll ask someone. Be right back."

He caught their server, their bill and Lovie's card still in hand. "My man, did you run that card yet?"

The server motioned to the wait station. "No, I'll do that right now. We've been slammed," he started to explain.

"Hey, no worries, look," Saxon glanced around, making sure Lovie wasn't watching. "Use this card and I'll take that one." He pulled his credit card out of his wallet and held it out.

The server reluctantly took the card and handed Lovie's card to Saxon.

Saxon watched as the server processed his card and had him sign the receipt. Saxon added a generous tip and placed both cards in his pocket.

When he reached the table, he remained standing, hoping to distract her. "You ready to head out? Thanks for dinner, by the way. I had a great time."

Lovie glanced up at him. "Oh, you're welcome, but we can't leave yet. I didn't get my card back."

He whipped it out of his pocket. "Sorry, here you go."

She stared at the card in his hand then back at him. "Why do you have my card?" her eyes narrowed. "You switched our cards, didn't you?"

Saxon shrugged, still holding her card out. "I might have. I couldn't let you pay for dinner. From what you've told me, I figured things are tight right now so I'm happy to treat."

Lovie took her card without touching his hand. "I wouldn't have offered to pay if I couldn't afford it."

Saxon could feel the tension between them rising. He wanted to explain that he was so used to taking control of situations that he often forgot to think about the other person's feelings. "I know that, but I still wanted to do something nice for you," he said, trying to diffuse the situation.

Lovie let out a heavy sigh. "I appreciate that, Saxon. I really do. But next time, just let me pay. I'm not a charity case. I don't want you to feel like you have to take care of me," she said, her voice tight.

They walked back to his car in silence.

Lovie spoke up. "Look, Saxon, I'm sorry if I overreacted back there. It's just that I hate feeling like I owe someone something," she said, her voice softening.

Saxon nodded, relieved that she was willing to talk about it. "I understand. I didn't mean to make you feel that way. I get the sense that you're used to putting everyone's needs above your own and I wanted to ease your burdens a bit," he said, hoping she would believe him.

"I appreciate it. It's just that I don't want anyone to think I'm helpless," she said after a long pause.

Saxon smiled. "I know you're not helpless. You're one of the most determined, persistent people I've ever met. But sometimes it's nice to let someone take care of you, even if it's just for a little while," he said, realizing that he wanted to see her succeed, wanted to see her happy.

Lovie stood still with her arms crossed, deep in thought. "It's been a while since anyone took care of me," she admitted softly. "Maybe I don't know what that looks like anymore."

Saxon felt a pang of regret that the evening was ending.

"Next time, I'll order one of everything on the menu and you can pay." he said, opening the car door for her.

Rolling her eyes, Lovie countered, "You do that and I'll be the one doing the switcheroo."

Saxon slid into the car and turned to her. "I really had a good time tonight."

She raised an eyebrow. "You sound surprised."

"My cousin Gia kind of dared me to try something new," he said. "As you probably can tell, I tend to go with the tried and true. She raved about this place and I wasn't sure I'd like it."

"The food was great, as was the company." She was staring at him, almost daring him to make a move. "I'm flattered that you got out of your comfort zone with me."

Without a second thought, he leaned over and pressed his lips to hers. She responded eagerly, her hand resting on his thigh.

Saxon felt a jolt of electricity run through his body as he kissed Lovie. He couldn't resist her any longer, and he knew he had to show her just how much he wanted her. His hand reached up to cup her cheek as he sucked on her bottom lip. Lovie responded in kind, pulling him in deeper and attempting to wrap her arms around his neck.

Suddenly Lovie yelped, releasing him. She tugged her seatbelt off. "Forgot I had that on," she muttered, rubbing her arms.

Saxon pulled away, his heart pounding in his chest. The reality that they were in the hotel parking lot making out like teenagers hit him and he grinned. He'd thought those days were long over.

"God, Lovie," he gasped, "I've been wanting to do that all night."

Lovie's eyes were dark with desire as she looked at him. "Me too," she whispered, before pulling him in for another kiss. "Even though I'm still low key annoyed that you went behind my back and paid for dinner," she murmured.

He fingered one of the curls framing her face. "What can I do to get off your shit list?"

She appeared to consider his question carefully. "More books," she said, her gaze meeting his. "And you can join me upstairs."

Saxon went still. He wanted nothing more than to spend the night with her but would she regret the decision in the morning? "Tonight? Are you sure?"

Shifting slightly, Lovie asked, "Are you trying to talk me out of it?"

Saxon shook his head. "Not at all, just making sure this isn't the margaritas talking."

At least he hoped it wasn't a liquor fueled desire on her part.

She let out a deep sigh. "You know that shirt you gave me to sleep in the other night?"

He nodded, wondering where this was going.

"Well, the shirt smells like you and I like wearing it while I...do things...by myself."

He frowned, then it hit him like a sledgehammer; his balls tightened at her words, and he swore that if she talked about him like that while they were doing the real thing, he'd never last a minute. "Can I see you in it again?"

"Depends," she said, shrugging her shoulders.

"Oh yeah? On what?" Saxon decided he liked this playful side of Lovie almost as much as the take charge businesswoman.

"Well," she said, her voice husky. "If you come to my hotel room and show me how much you like it on me, I might let you take it off."

CHAPTER 8

Lovie

Lovie stood, alone, waiting for the elevator.

She'd asked Saxon to give her a few minutes before he came up.

Part of her wanted to tell him she was just kidding, and part of her wanted him more than anything else in the world.

What made her so bold in the car?

The words slipped out before she could twist them, run them through her common sense filter. Maybe it was the margaritas talking. Her skin warmed. She hadn't meant to tell him about his shirt but Saxon brought out her inner sex kitten. She wasn't aware she had one until he'd laid those sexy brown eyes on her.

Eyes that reflected unequivocal desire for her.

God, she wanted him.

The elevator sounded and the doors slid open. She waited as a pair of teenaged girls burst out, so engrossed in something on one's phone that they nearly collided with her. "Sorry," one muttered as they hurried toward the lobby.

She tapped the number three button and willed the doors closed before anyone else came along.

Her nerves were shifting into overdrive. What if he changed

his mind? Worst yet, what if he was one of those men that got theirs and snuck out before the sun rose?

What if he called her Sloane?

It wouldn't be first time she'd been called some other woman's name on the brink of her release.

Maybe she should tell him she changed her mind.

The elevator doors opened and Lovie hustled toward her room.

Once she was in the quiet stillness of her room, she turned on a lamp and picked her phone up, debating on sending him a text to call the whole thing off.

Just in case he did show up, she decided to take a quick shower.

After her shower, Lovie undid her hair, letting it flow in loose waves over one shoulder and she slipped on the t-shirt. She loved the softness of it against her skin.

She checked her phone. Nothing from Saxon.

Lovie paced the small room, making a deal. If he wasn't knocking on her door within the next ten minutes, she'd send him a text telling him good night.

There was a knock at the door.

Lovie's heart skipped a beat. She took a deep breath, trying to calm her nerves, and opened the door.

Saxon stood there, looking as handsome as ever, holding a small stuffed animal that looked oddly like a snake. She stepped aside so he could enter then closed the door.

His gaze roamed her body and her nipples tightened shamelessly in response. She crossed her arms over them and motioned at the stuffed animal. "What's that?"

Saxon blinked, then looked at the object in his hand like he'd never seen it before. "This is," he peered at the attached tag, "Wordsworth. He's a bookworm, get it?"

Sure enough, as Lovie turned the plush animal around, she saw it was a worm, not a snake, and sported a pair of owlish glasses.

No one besides her nieces had ever given her a stuffed animal before.

This man was dangerously close to making her believe in love again.

Lovie smiled at the sight of the stuffed animal. Saxon was full of surprises. "You calling me a book nerd?" she asked, chuckling. "He's cute, thank you." She placed it on the bed.

Saxon stepped closer to her, his eyes darkening with desire. "Sexiest book nerd ever. You look better in that shirt than I ever would, Lovie," he said, his voice deep, almost a whisper. "God, you're beautiful. I don't know if I want to take this shirt off you. Not yet anyway."

Her heart soared, whisking away her doubts and reservations. She leaned in, snaking her arms around his neck as she kissed him deeply.

Saxon's hands explored her back, grazing over her hips, tugging her closer still.

Lovie moaned into his mouth, her body humming with pleasure. She could feel his erection pressing against her and the urge to touch him, to be skin on skin with him almost overwhelmed her.

The Book Barrel t-shirt's length left most of Lovie's thighs exposed and Saxon's hands lingered briefly at the hem of the shirt before venturing underneath.

Lovie's eyes fluttered closed.

She felt his deep growl when he realized she wasn't wearing anything underneath the shirt.

He broke their kiss. "You're killing me, Lovie, you feel that, right?"

She couldn't have answered if her life depended on it.

Saxon lifted her up, dropping her on the bed.

He raised the shirt, exposing her heated body to the chill in the room and Lovie shuddered. Before she could protest, Saxon had positioned himself between her thighs as he took a hard puckered nipple in his mouth.

Lovie cried out, arching into his hands and mouth.

Needing to touch him, Lovie made quick work of his belt and fly, freeing him, and he moaned around her breast as she stroked him.

Saxon released her nipple and trailed kisses along her middle, dipping his tongue into her navel, then continuing lower. Lovie writhed in anticipation, her breath coming in soft gasps.

He dipped his head as his hot tongue explored her wet heat and Lovie whimpered, raising her hips to meet his mouth.

Her hips bucked as he licked and sucked, thrusting his tongue inside her, teasing her with his lips and teeth.

Lovie's hands wound around his head. "Oh, god, Saxon. Yes." His mouth was so warm and wet. "Yes."

Lovie bit into her lower lip, attempting to stifle her cries. He was driving her over the edge and she was powerless to stop it. Her body began to shake and she felt the tingle in every nerve ending.

Over the edge she tumbled, crying his name as the force of her orgasm overtook her.

When she could once again form a coherent thought, she reached for him.

"Saxon, I want you inside me," she panted, her breath coming in gasps.

He obliged, pausing only to grab a condom from his wallet.

Her legs wrapped around his waist as he thrust deep inside her, his thick shaft filling her, taking her.

Each stroke had her crying out and arching into his hands.

"Tell me what you need."

"You. You're everything I need," she said, driving her hips up to meet his.

"You feel so good, Lovie," Saxon groaned. "So fucking good."

Lovie felt her body tensing as Saxon thrust, pushing her closer and closer. "I'm so close," she whispered, barely able to get the words out.

"Come for me, baby."

Lovie cried out and as her body began to shake, Saxon

smothered her cries with his lips, taking her mouth as he continued to thrust inside her. The sensation was too much and Lovie could feel herself unraveling, pleasure washing over her in waves. Her back arched and she held onto him tighter as the orgasm shattered through her.

Saxon stiffened and he growled as he came, his release sending a ripple of aftershocks through Lovie's body.

He collapsed on top of her, and for a few minutes, neither of them moved. Lovie sighed with contentment as she listened to Saxon's heart beat.

After a quick detour to the bathroom, Saxon collapsed onto the bed beside her then pulled her into his arms. He pressed a sloppy, wet kiss on her forehead. "I blame the shirt," he said, his voice hoarse.

Lovie woke up to find the room filled with a soft, golden light. She glanced around in confusion, wondering for a moment where she was.

She was still in Kissing Springs. With Saxon.

He was out of bed, getting dressed.

"Hey," he said quietly, "I've got to get the store ready to open."

She stretched then nodded. Reality came crashing back. They both had jobs to do.

Saxon sat on the edge of the bed, pulling on his shoes. "What's your day look like?"

Yawning, Lovie sat up. "Golf course all day. I'm going to shoot a bunch of videos and then create some short clips I can use on social media."

"Sounds like you've got a full day ahead. I'll call you later on." He kissed her quickly and before she could say anything more, he was gone.

Refusing to sink into her feelings and pout because Saxon was gone, Lovie pulled herself out of bed and made her way to the bathroom.

Lovie checked the time. She was touring the golf course today for footage she could use in her social media campaigns. Later she'd draft some press releases and talk to some media contacts.

Grabbing her laptop bag and purse, Lovie started to head out of her room.

She stopped, picked up the stuffed bookworm and dropped him into her purse.

Her busy schedule meant she didn't have time to reflect on her evening with Saxon but she found herself thinking about him at random times during her day. Did he play golf? She wouldn't be surprised if he did. He liked the finer things in life and she could see him being as comfortable on a golf course as he was sipping bourbon in his shop.

The morning went by quickly. Lovie took a quick break to eat lunch and was finishing off a chicken salad sandwich when her sister Layla called.

Lovie finished her lunch and washed it down with a glass of ice cold lemonade before calling Layla back.

"Hey, how's the golf course tour going?" Layla asked.

"Good, I could definitely use your organization skills with this project," Lovie said, glancing at her to do list. "There's a ton of work to be done."

There was a pause and Lovie could tell her sister was considering the idea. "I've never worked at a golf course. I know nothing about golf," she said.

Lovie smiled and shook her head. "I'm not asking you to be an instructor. It's really just project management, which you're great at. It would be much easier if I had someone else to help me out," she admitted.

"Well, that's why I was calling, ok let me not lie...I called to get the tea on your night. Your niece wanted to talk and you didn't answer, but let's get business out of the way first."

Lovie's face got warm. She had been wrapped up with Saxon

when they called and she'd meant to call back but she'd been distracted.

"Yes, business first. Aren't the girls out of school next week?"

"They are, I swear these kids are out of school more than they're in. But yes, it's autumn break and I was thinking we could all come to Kentucky for the week so I can help you. Not sure what we'll do with the kids during the day but I'll figure something out."

Lovie stopped eating, thinking through the possibilities. Yes, having Layla around to help would be great, especially with the signing next week. Maybe she could find a vacation house for the week so they'd have more room and a full kitchen.

"Yeah, you all should come. Hey, Lay, if you get a chance, could you look for a place to rent for the week?"

"Sure thing. So...what did you do last night?"

Lovie rolled her eyes but couldn't stop the smile that crossed her face. She'd hoped to distract Layla from asking about her evening. She was still processing it herself. Lovie hesitated before answering her sister. "I asked him up to my hotel room. We were both sober and that's all I'll say."

Layla laughed. "Girl, whatever...I can hear through the phone that you're grinning so I'm gonna assume he handled business and you got a good after sex glow going on today."

Lovie tried to keep her voice level. "I don't."

Layla's laughter only increased. "Mm-hmm. Was it good?"

An involuntary shudder of pleasure passed through her as she considered their evening.

"Better than good," Lovie said finally with a sigh, "Amazing actually."

"Yep, I know you and I know you're glowing. Good for you. I'm glad one of us hasn't lost her faith in love."

Lovie could hear the wistfulness in her sister's voice.

"You just need time to heal your heart. Every man isn't like Kent."

Layla grunted. "I know that on some level but I'm not

willing to chance it anymore. Anyway, enough about me. Go be amazing on the golf course. I'm gonna go prep for yet another job interview in a few minutes. I'm overqualified for the job and I'm sure they'll ghost me when I give them my salary requirements."

"Well, good luck anyway. We'll talk later. Love you, sis!"

She ended the call and dropped the phone into her purse. Lovie wished she had enough clients to support bringing her sister on full time but she wasn't there yet. Maybe she'd suggest Layla apply at some of the local businesses in Kissing Springs. She'd ask Saxon about that.

Saxon. Thinking about him made her smile. Lovie pulled a compact mirror from her purse. Layla was wrong; she didn't have any sex glow or whatever she'd called it, not that she saw anyway. She applied a new coat of lip gloss and snapped the compact shut. Yes, she missed him but this thing between them wasn't a big deal. Once her jobs were finished, she'd head back to Charlotte and Saxon would be here running his store.

Lovie ignored the hint of panic running through her.

She was taking a video of the on-site restaurant when Stan rolled up in a sleek golf cart. "Hey, Lovie! I heard you were filming today," he called out. "You need any shots of me?"

Lovie aimed her phone at him, capturing the golf cart and Stan hamming it up for the camera.

"Sure, you look ready to hit the links this morning."

He smiled and posed for her then stepped out of the golf cart. "I wish. Actually, I've been sitting in the pro shop all morning. Filing paperwork." He winced. "I hate paperwork."

"How's the course looking? You get some good footage?" he asked as he surveyed the dining area.

The golf course was in the final stages of being crafted into a golfer's dream. It was nestled on the outskirts of Kissing Springs and had stunning views of rolling hills. The clubhouse was a log cabin with modern amenities. The place exuded luxury in a rugged way.

"Yep. I've got lots to work with. I'll edit the videos tonight when I get back to my hotel room."

"You know, I had a last minute cancellation at our vacation house if you're tired of staying in a hotel. It's available for the rest of the month. They had to pretty much pay for the whole reservation so it's yours, I just need the cost of the cleaning crew to get it ready for the next guests."

"That's really nice of you to offer," Lovie said. She'd been trying to save some money on her trip and a free place to stay would be great. Plus it would be nice to have a real kitchen she could cook in instead of relying on takeout every night. "I'd love to try it out, if you're sure that's okay."

Stan waved away her concerns. "Of course, it's no problem at all. I'll text you the address and send the cleaning crew out right away so it should be all ready when you get there."

Stan's phone rang loudly. "Well, duty calls. Call me if you need anything."

With that, he strode back outside toward the golf cart.

Lovie couldn't wait to share the news with Layla. She knew her sister could use a change of scenery and some time away from her current struggles.

As she wrapped up her work day, she realized that Layla would be meeting Saxon for the first time when she and the girls came to town. What would her sister think of him? And what would she do if the two of them didn't get along?

CHAPTER 9

Saxon

Saxon whistled as he restocked the children's section displays with Halloween themed titles. Every year, the store did a big Halloween party for the children of Kissing Springs complete with a costume contest, story hour, trick or treat alley, and fun Halloween movie screenings.

Based on the sunny day outside, he wouldn't know Halloween was the following month. The sky was a brilliant blue with few clouds. A perfect day to be outside enjoying the mild weather.

Which, it seemed, was what everyone was doing. The store was quiet; most of the residents of Kissing Springs were at the annual Taste of Kissing Springs festival in the heart of downtown.

He glanced at the time on a large wall clock in the rear of the store. Normally he closed every day at six, another two hours from then. Maybe he'd close an hour early and head over to the festival.

Lovie might want to join him for a tour of downtown. He could take her to see his cousin Jameson's gym and Gia's lingerie boutique.

He paused. If he introduced her to the family, they'd get the wrong idea. He hadn't introduced them to anyone he dated since his divorce and they'd make a big deal out of it, especially his Aunt Carla.

Now that Jameson was happily married, she'd made it her mission to encourage him to get back out there and date again.

Did he dare let his extended family meet her? They'd be planning his wedding along with Gia's if he wasn't careful.

Saxon thought about her smile and the way her eyes lit up when he gifted her the thriller novel. They had that love of books in common and he couldn't wait to see what she thought of the book.

He couldn't wait to see her. Period.

He picked up his phone.

"Hey, Lovie," Saxon said as soon as she answered.

Lovie's voice was soft on the other end. "Hey, Saxon. What's up?"

"What are your thoughts on sampling all the different foods Kissing Springs has to offer then jumping on a hastily constructed carnival ride?

There was silence on the other end. "My thoughts? The first part, yes. The second...maybe not. What's up?"

"I'm closing the store early today and heading over to the Taste of Kissing Springs festival. Care to join me? I'll nix the rides and we could do a tour of downtown together."

"Hmm, I had an exciting evening of wine and takeout planned but I'm intrigued. I'd love to join you."

Saxon was surprised by how eager he was to show off his town to Lovie. He had been excited before, but now he was almost giddy with anticipation. He felt like a schoolkid on the first day of summer vacation as he rushed up to his apartment after closing the store to change into a pair of jeans and a casual shirt suitable for an afternoon at the festival.

When he arrived at her hotel, Lovie was already waiting for him in the lobby. She was wearing a light blue denim skirt that gave him a tantalizing view of her long legs and an emerald green blouse. Her long ebony hair was pulled into a side braid. She looked amazing and Saxon wasn't sure he'd be able to keep his hands off her while they were in public. Maybe this wasn't such a good idea.

"Hey," Saxon said, forcing himself to smile. He felt like he was leering.

"What's wrong? Am I dressed ok for a festival? I've never been to one and I didn't really pack much in terms of casual wear..." she trailed off.

He pulled her toward him, kissing her lightly on the lips. "You look good enough to eat. We should go before I change my mind and drag you back to your room for a repeat of last night."

"You look pretty good yourself," Lovie said with a cheeky grin. "But yeah, we should go."

Saxon chuckled and took her hand, leading her out of the hotel and towards his car.

"Wait, did I hear you right? You've never been to a festival?" he asked once they were on the road.

"Nope. My parents worked a lot and my dad always told us that carnivals and the like were prime hunting grounds for people looking to abduct kids. He basically scared us from ever wanting to go."

Saxon took his eyes off the road to study her briefly. "So what made you want to come with me?"

Lovie shrugged. "I figure it's a small town event so low risk of abduction and my curiosity got the best of me. I want to experience more of Kissing Springs."

Saxon chuckled at her response. "Well, I'm not going to let anything happen to you. Kissing Springs is a great town and the festival is relatively new, but it's grown every year. You'll love it."

As they pulled into the parking lot, Lovie's eyes widened at the sight of the colorful tents and vendors setting up. The aroma of different foods wafted through the air and Saxon's stomach growled loudly.

"Where should we start?" Lovie asked, her eyes scanning the area.

"We'll get food first then we can do bourbon samples. I know just the place," Saxon said, taking her hand and leading her towards a food stand that was known for its famous pulled pork sandwiches.

As they waited in line, Saxon stole glances at Lovie. She was radiating with excitement and her smile could light up the entire festival. He knew he was in deep when he found himself wanting to show her all the things he loved about his town.

When they finally got their sandwiches, they wandered around, looking for an open table.

"Sax!" A voice called out. "Over here!"

Saxon's face lit up when he saw his cousin and uncle. He held a hand up in acknowledgment and Lovie followed him, her hand still in his.

They were seated at one of the picnic tables nearest the stage. A local band was due on any moment.

Jameson Mitchell stood and slapped hands with Saxon then pulled him into a man hug. "What's up, man?"

Saxon embraced his Uncle Charlie as well and was about to ask where his Aunt Carla was when Jameson nudged him in the ribs. "You gonna introduce us to your lady friend?"

"Of course. Lovie, this is my cousin Jameson and my Uncle Charlie. This is Lovie, she's a publicist in town promoting Sloane's new book."

Jameson lifted a brow at Saxon. "Sloane's book, huh? Nice to meet you, Lovie." He shook Lovie's hand. "I trust Saxon has taken his head out of his books long enough to show you around town?"

She smiled at Jameson. "Yes, he's been a great host."

Saxon sat down next to Lovie and handed her one of the pulled pork sandwiches he'd bought earlier. As they ate, Saxon felt Jameson's intense gaze and refused to meet his eye. "Where's your wife, Jay?"

Jameson glanced around. "They're here somewhere. Gia's dragging her around the dessert vendors. They both have wedding fever right now." He looked at Lovie. "My sister Gia just got engaged. She should be back soon."

"Oh, I'd love to meet her," she turned to Saxon. "The pork is spicy, where can I get something besides bourbon to drink?" Lovie asked.

Jameson pointed to a local vendor and she hurried off to the tent.

He watched her purchase the water then she wandered to another table where pastries and other desserts were on display.

He heard Jameson clear his throat behind him and he turned toward the man he'd always considered an older brother.

"So you're messing around with Sloane's publicist now?"

Saxon tensed at Jameson's words, his jaw clenching. "We're just hanging out. It's nothing serious."

Jameson raised an eyebrow. "Uh-huh. You haven't taken your eyes off her since you all got here."

Saxon scowled at Jameson. "She's never been to anything like this before. Just making sure she's good. That's all." Was he trying to convince himself as well?

"You say so," Jameson shrugged. "Just noticed this is the first woman we're meeting since you and Sloane parted ways. Just sayin'."

"You're reading more into this than you need to." Saxon glanced over at Uncle Charlie, hoping for an ally, but the older man merely shrugged.

"Can't say I blame him, son. She's a looker, that one," Uncle Charlie said.

"Look, I like Lovie, okay?" Saxon said, his voice low. "I just don't want to rush things and have everyone jumping to conclusions."

Jameson studied him for a long moment before nodding. "All right, man. Just be careful, okay? You tend to go all in head first when you find something or someone you want."

Saxon clenched his fists, feeling a flash of anger and pain.

"I know, Jay. I'm taking it slow," Saxon replied, his voice strained. "But I appreciate your concern."

Just then, Gia arrived at the table, followed by Noemie, and his Aunt Carla. "Saxon! You must have closed the store early." Gia threw her arms around him.

"Yeah, everybody in town is here so no point in staying open. I think next year I'll rent a booth for the whole weekend instead of just the one day."

Gia nodded. "Yeah, same here. I got a booth for Saturday only, but there's plenty of people here for a Friday night."

Gia owned a lingerie boutique downtown not far from where the festival was being held.

Lovie returned then, a huge grin on her face. "I got fried Oreos!"

Gia stopped, her eyes sliding over to Saxon's. He saw the speculation in them and knew Gia would evaluate Lovie's every move.

"Lovie, this is my cousin Gia. Gia, this is Lovie," he said hastily.

"Nice to meet you, Lovie. You new in town or just visiting?"

"Business actually, I'm Sloane St. James' publicist." Lovie stuck out her hand and shook Gia's.

"Oh, right, Sloane changed her name again."

"Really? I figured Sloane St. James was a pen name, but that's her actual name? I haven't met her in person yet." Lovie sipped her water.

Gia chuckled. "Well, that should be interesting. Sloane is an intriguing character. How'd you end up as her publicist?"

"Her publisher reached out to me. I've been working with them and we're kicking off her book tour at Saxon's shop."

Saxon frowned. He hadn't shared that with any of the family yet.

His Aunt Carla cocked an eyebrow then turned to Lovie with a warm smile. "Hey Lovie, nice to meet you, I'm Carla, Saxon's aunt."

Lovie shook the older woman's hand.

Gia swung her head towards him. "Oh, is that right? You're letting your ex-wife do a book signing at your store?"

"Yes. The publicity will help both of us."

Sighing, Gia put a hand on his arm. "Just be careful, Saxon. I don't trust her."

Why was everyone acting like he was some delicate being that needed protection?

Saxon brushed off Gia's warning. "I can handle Sloane. It's strictly business."

Gia gave him a skeptical look before turning to Lovie. "So, what do you think of our little town so far?"

Lovie smiled. "I love it. The festival is amazing and everyone has been so welcoming."

"That's great to hear. You should come back for our Christmas celebration. It's the biggest event of the year."

Noemie hopped up, a set of keys jingling in her hand. "Anybody want to use a real ladies room? I'll go open the gym."

Gia stood. "Yes, please," She turned to Lovie. "You want to come to my brother's gym with us? The facilities are much nicer than the portable toilets here."

Lovie nodded and the women set off for Main Street where J&J Fitness was located.

As the women walked away, Saxon felt a sense of relief. He was glad that Lovie was getting along with his family, but he knew they wouldn't immediately warm to any woman he brought home. Sloane had done a number on all of them. He knew that he was not ready to jump into anything serious just yet, but his heart fluttered every time he caught a glimpse of Lovie.

His Uncle Charlie laid a hand on his arm. "Does Sloane know you and Lovie are together?"

"We're hanging out. Nothing serious."

Jameson snorted behind him. "Says you. She's got you wrapped around her pinkie. Welcome to the club."

Saxon eyed his cousin. "What club?"

"The Fool in Love club," Jameson replied with a smirk.

Saxon rolled his eyes. "I'm not in love. She's fun to hang around, that's all."

Uncle Charlie chuckled. "Sure thing, Saxon. We believe you."

"Remember this day, dad," Jameson smirked. "We'll wait for you to catch up."

Saxon rolled his eyes. Sometimes Jameson acted like he knew everything.

Later, after the rest of the family left, Lovie and Saxon strolled down the main strip, eating waffle cones full of homemade ice cream from one of the vendors.

"You having fun? How was your first festival?" Saxon asked, motioning to a bench under a large tree in the town square.

"Oh," Lovie flopped down onto the bench, patting her stomach with her free hand. "I've eaten too much and I'm a touch tipsy from all the bourbon tastings but this was great. And your family was so nice to me. Your cousin even invited me to her wedding."

Saxon dumped the last of his ice cream and took a seat beside Lovie.

She licked the side of her cone to catch the melting ice cream as Saxon watched, mesmerized.

"Damn...what I wouldn't give to be that waffle cone right now," he murmured.

Lovie stopped, looked up at him, a slow smile on her face. "You want ice cream all over you too?"

"You're kinda freaky," he said, rubbing a drop of ice cream from the corner of her mouth with his thumb. "I like it."

Saxon licked the ice cream off his thumb then leaned in and kissed her, his hands sliding down to her waist. She tasted like sweet cream and sugar, and he couldn't get enough of her. They broke apart, breathing heavily, and Lovie gazed at him, heat flashing in her eyes.

Saxon captured her mouth again, eager to hear that deep

moan she made when she was aroused. He pushed her back against the bench, his hands trailing down to her thighs.

She wrapped her arms around his neck, pulling him closer as they kissed hungrily. Saxon's hands roamed over her legs creeping under the denim skirt. He couldn't believe how much she turned him on, how much he wanted her.

"Saxon?"

He froze. Saxon groaned inwardly as he heard the voice behind him.

Lovie let out a short huff and scooted back to her side of the bench.

He sighed. "Sloane. Your timing, as usual, leaves much to be desired."

CHAPTER 10

Lovie

Lovie gasped then tugged at her skirt again. It seemed longer when she'd put it on, but she felt exposed in the damn thing. Seconds ago, she'd been ready to straddle Saxon in the middle of Main Street, now she was face-to-face with her new client and a man, presumably her client's date, that was smirking at her. Lovie stood, her eyes on the woman.

She finally got to meet Saxon's ex-wife.

Sloane St. James was shorter than Lovie expected. Sloane couldn't have been more than an inch or two over five feet, Lovie guessed. She towered over the slender, well-dressed woman, she realized, and maybe should have remained seated.

Sloane was everything Lovie wasn't: delicate, thin and fair skinned with naturally wavy shoulder length hair.

The four were silent, each couple appraising the other.

Sloane was staring at her as if she wanted an explanation or an apology.

Lovie spoke up first. "Sloane, I'm Lovie, nice to meet you."

Sloane's mouth dropped slightly. "Oh, you move fast, don't you?" she drawled, sounding like a Kentucky belle. "No wonder Saxon agreed to the signing so quickly."

Saxon stood, "Sloane..."

She held up a hand. "Calm down, I'm only joking. I think it's good that you found someone, Saxon." She touched his arm as if to reassure him, and Lovie felt a flash of jealousy.

Sloane grabbed the man's hand "This is Tarik. Tarik, meet my ex and Lovie, my publicist."

Tarik shook their hands then stepped back, putting a possessive hand on Sloane's back.

Watching the pair, Lovie had to admit Sloane and Tarik made a handsome couple. Tarik was Lovie's height and muscular like a boxer with deep brown skin and a smooth bald head. He was nice looking, she decided. Not as sexy as Saxon, but Lovie assumed he turned many heads when he entered a room.

"You're a publicist?" Tarik addressed her.

"Yes, and social media strategist." She whipped out a business card and handed it to him. She'd gotten about a thousand cards printed and she was determined to use them.

"I could use your services. I run a real estate investment and renovation company. We want to start running ads on social media."

"Darling, you know Lovie is in charge of my book tour, she might not have time to take on another client just yet," Sloane said lightly.

"Actually I'm bringing my sister on to help me so I may be able to assist," Lovie said.

"Lovie is also doing the PR for Stan's golf course," Saxon said, and Lovie couldn't tell if he was boasting or simply stating a fact.

"You're in town for a while, right, Lovie?" She didn't wait for a response. "Why don't the four of us have dinner tomorrow night?"

Saxon glanced at Lovie then rubbed his neck. "I'm running a tent for the festival tomorrow."

"What about Sunday? The festival will be over. Besides, Tarik has an idea he wants to run by you." Sloane touched his arm again and Lovie noticed Tarik's jaw tighten. "And he and Lovie can talk about marketing while we discuss my signing. It's perfect."

Lovie immediately knew Sloane St. James was used to getting her way. She'd made that last statement like everything was settled and the three of them would fall in line.

Saxon turned to her. "Are you free Sunday night?" he asked. She couldn't read Saxon's expression. Should she decline? She would have preferred they discuss business during the day over lunch but having dinner with Saxon was a perk.

"Um, sure. Dinner sounds good."

His shoulders relaxed slightly and he gave her a grateful smile.

Tarik's arm went around Sloane's waist. "It's settled then."

"Yes, we can go to the Skeleton Bar in Rodey. Lovie, would you mind making us a reservation?"

Saxon huffed. "I'll call Bristol, I get a lot of bourbon from their distillery."

Lovie watched the men. There was a weird energy between Saxon and Tarik, something beyond each sizing the other man up. She wondered if it was just her imagination, or if there was more to this dinner than just discussing business. But she pushed the thought aside, telling herself that she was being paranoid. She didn't want to ruin the opportunity to network with Tarik and potentially gain another client.

As the group parted ways, Lovie walked with Saxon towards his vehicle. She wanted to know what was on his mind. "Is everything okay?" she finally asked, breaking the silence.

Saxon shrugged. "I can't explain it. I've never met Tarik before tonight. But something about him rubs me the wrong way."

"I could tell," Lovie said, getting into the passenger seat. "Are you sure you want to do dinner with them?"

He snorted, leaving the car off. "I'd rather spend the evening with my accountant explaining tax code to me."

Lovie winced.

"Exactly," Saxon chuckled. "The man is brilliant at what he does but he's long winded and way too excited about taxes. However, as much as I would rather spend Sunday evening alone with you, if I don't do this dinner, then Sloane will make the signing miserable for both of us."

Lovie had picked up on Sloane's subtle dig at her even though she'd assured them she was joking. She knew to keep her guard up around women like Sloane. "How so? The signing is for her benefit."

"Nothing will be right, from the temperature in the store to the sparkling water not being her favorite brand," he sighed and started the car. "And she'll treat you like you're her personal servant. But having said that, I understand if you don't want to go to dinner with her and Real Estate Ralph."

Lovie hooted with laughter. "Real Estate Ralph?"

"Yep, didn't he seem like a bro that would be doing You Tube videos from a rented yacht trying to convince his followers that he's the next Warren Buffet?"

"Yeah," she moved her hand in a "maybe so" motion. "I could see that. But I'm curious about his business proposal. I don't mind going, that is if you want me to."

"Thank you. Hopefully it will be drama-free."

Lovie and Saxon arrived at the Skeleton Bar a few minutes early and took seats at the bar to wait for Sloane and Tarik.

"Sloane was born two days after her due date and has been late to almost everything since then so you might as well order a drink while we wait." Saxon's voice was tinged with sarcasm.

Lovie smiled at Saxon's comment and ordered a glass of red wine. She took a sip and looked around the bar. It was dimly lit, with a cozy and intimate atmosphere.

She turned to Saxon, "What's the matter? You seem really tense. Is there something you're not telling me?"

Saxon clenched his jaw, "I just have a bad feeling about this. I don't trust Tarik."

Lovie furrowed her brows, "Why not?"

"I don't know. Call it a gut feeling. He's too possessive of Sloane. Something about the way he looks at you makes me uncomfortable. Just be careful around him, okay?" Saxon's eyes bored into hers, a seriousness in his tone.

Lovie nodded, taking a sip of her drink. "Okay. I'll keep that in mind."

As they finished their drinks, Sloane and Tarik walked in and joined them at the bar.

Sloane walked in with her head held high and her arm linked with Tarik's. He whispered something into her ear, causing her to laugh and nuzzle into his chest. Lovie thought the motion a little forced, like they were playing nice for the people watching.

Tarik was dressed in a dark blue suit that hugged his muscular frame perfectly. His bald head shone under the dim lights, and Lovie found herself thinking of Saxon's cautionary words. Be careful around him.

"Hey, guys!" Sloane chirped, interrupting Lovie's thoughts. "Sorry we're late. Tarik had to take a call from one of his investors."

"No worries," Saxon said, a forced smile on his lips. "Shall we get a table?"

The four of them settled into a booth in the corner of the bar. Saxon took Lovie's hand under the table, his thumb absently caressing her skin as they talked.

The gesture calmed her and she tried to relax. Sloane reminded Lovie of the girls in high school who'd bullied her. She'd been too much in their eyes: too tall, too dark, too fat, and they'd attempted to make her life as miserable as their own.

Their server greeted them, pouring ice water into their glasses and described the specials for that evening then said she'd check back to take drink orders.

"Even though this is basically a small, one-horse town, I love the food here. And I was able to get Lockland bourbon in Saxon's bookstore." Sloane said, smirking at Saxon. She turned to Lovie. "I did a brief stint as a real estate agent while we were still married," she explained. "I was able to learn the ropes from a woman on the brink of retiring and I took what she told me and ran with it. Top seller for twelve consecutive months."

Lovie leaned in. She hadn't known this about Sloane. "Wow, you must be a fast learner. What inspired you to start writing?"

"Well, marriage is hard, especially when we women don't fully know ourselves or what we want or how we want to be loved. We expect our men to be everything we need and complete us, but we have to be whole first." Sloane paused to sip her water. "I expected Saxon to read my mind and know how neglected I felt when he was spending time at the store but I didn't communicate that well."

Saxon raised his eyes to meet Sloane's. "I think you wrote enough about our marriage in your book; why don't we talk about something else?"

Sloane smiled sweetly. "Ah, so you have read my book."

Saxon looked like he was going to say something and Lovie could tell it wasn't going to be complimentary. "Tarik, do you work with residential or commercial properties?"

Tarik gave a tight smile and leaned back, folding his arms over his chest. "I work with both, but I specialize in commercial real estate. I'm currently developing a high-end shopping center in Seattle."

Lovie listened as Tarik described the development and what it entailed. He was passionate about his work and she could tell he enjoyed talking about it. Sloane seemed interested too, though her eyes kept darting between Saxon and Tarik, as if she were expecting them to jump up and fight at any moment.

Sloane snaked an arm through Tarik's. "He's such a genius when it comes to negotiating deals."

She looked at Lovie. "He's going to start taking on clients, people who want to get into real estate investing, so if you're interested, Lovie, now's the time."

Tarik nodded. "And that's what I wanted to conversate with you about, Saxon. We're looking to bring in investors for this all-inclusive resort we're doing in Jamaica. Luxury all the way. It's going to be a huge five-star property right on the beach."

Lovie caught Saxon's impatient sigh at Tarik's sales pitch. "Are you building it from the ground up or renovating a current property?" Saxon asked.

"Ground up. Totally new construction," Tarik responded promptly. "Like nothing they've seen before. The top floor will be a huge penthouse style suite complete with butlers."

Lovie could tell he was proud of the project, but Saxon looked doubtful.

"Most all-inclusive resorts harm rather than help local economies because guests tend to stay on the resort instead of venturing out and spending money with local vendors. How do you plan to benefit the local Jamaican community?"

Tarik scowled. "We're bringing jobs to the area. And we'll need local suppliers. This will be a win-win for everyone."

"Interesting. I'm not looking to invest in real estate right now, but good luck." Saxon was dismissive.

Tarik's smile didn't reach his eyes, Lovie noticed. He almost looked like he'd taken Saxon's questions personally. He took a sip of water. "This coming from a man that damn near stole that bookstore from a desperate old man."

Lovie's head shot up and she frowned at Saxon, who was turning a deep shade of red.

Sloane's eyes widened. "Why don't we order? Anybody else starving?"

"What did you just say?" Saxon's voice was steel.

Tarik's eyes bored into him. "I didn't stutter. You heard what I said."

Saxon eyed Sloane, who had an arm on Tarik. "What lies have you been spreading?"

Lovie could feel the tension in the air, thick and palpable. She looked at Saxon, whose face was contorted with anger. Sloane looked guilty, and Tarik's expression was one of smugness.

"What are you talking about?" The confidence Sloane radiated earlier was gone.

"Don't play dumb with me, Sloane. What lies did you tell Tarik about me?" Saxon's voice was low and dangerous.

Tarik leaned forward, his eyes gleaming with malice. "She told me that you manipulated an old man into selling you his bookstore for pennies on the dollar. That poor man had no idea what he was signing."

Saxon's fists clenched on the table, and Lovie could feel his rage radiating off him. "That's not true. I gave him a fair price for the store. He was happy with the deal."

Tarik snorted. "Sure he was. You're sitting over there, all high and mighty, dismissing my investment proposal like I'm some scammer while you took advantage of his desperation. You're a liar and a fraud, no better than the rest of us."

Lovie could see Saxon struggling to control his emotions. She could tell Tarik had struck a nerve. "I didn't manipulate anyone."

Sloane had gone quiet, her eyes darting between Saxon and Tarik. Lovie watched the panic take over her face. "Why are we still talking about this? Everyone got what they wanted. Saxon has his precious store," she turned to Lovie. "Don't be fooled. He'll act like he cares about you but if he has to choose between you and the damned store, well, you see how well that worked out for me."

Saxon stood up so suddenly that the table shook. "I don't have to listen to this. We're leaving." He grabbed Lovie's hand and pulled her towards the exit, not even looking back at Sloane and Tarik.

Lovie stumbled after him, her heart racing with adrenaline. As they stepped out into the cool night air, Saxon stopped abruptly and turned to face her.

"I'm sorry you had to witness that," he said, his voice shaking with anger.

"It's okay," Lovie replied, still trying to catch her breath. "Why does he think you cheated the former store owner?"

"I never took advantage of Mr. Mohr," Saxon continued, his voice strained. "The store needed a lot of work and we negotiated a fair price. He was happy with it. As you saw, Sloane has always been bitter about the bookstore. She swears I chose the store over her but she's wrong."

Lovie nodded, trying to imagine the hurt and anger Saxon must be feeling. She wanted to comfort him, but she didn't know how.

"I'm sorry," she said softly.

Saxon turned to her. "It's not your fault. I just wish she would stop spreading lies about me."

Lovie took a step closer to him, placing a hand on his arm. "I believe you," she said firmly.

He looked at her, and for a moment, they stood there in silence, their eyes locked. Lovie felt a spark of electricity between them, and she realized she was falling for him, despite everything that had happened.

Saxon stroked his beard. "I'm canceling that book signing."

CHAPTER 11

Saxon

Lovie took a step backward. "You can't cancel the signing...it's a week away. Everything's planned."

There was a tremor in her voice and he started to say he was joking but he couldn't.

He started to explain. "Lovie, I can't...

How could he make her see what being around Sloane did to him without sounding like he was weak? And what if she no longer wanted him in that state? No woman wanted a man she perceived as weak.

"I'm not doing the signing." he sighed deeply. "I know this is going to cost you but..."

"Do you? Saxon, I've got a lot riding on Sloane's book tour. Please don't cancel. The terms of the book tour are that your store is the kick-off. If we don't do the signing, the whole tour is off." Lovie was breathing heavily, her arms at her sides. "I need this tour, Saxon."

Saxon sighed again, running a hand over his head. He knew Lovie was right; she had put so much effort into this book tour and it would be a huge financial blow to her if he canceled. But he couldn't bear the thought of facing Sloane again, especially after the scene at dinner. He felt like he was losing control, and it terrified him.

"You have to understand, I'm tired. I'm tired of dealing with Sloane's BS. I can't spend another second in her presence and it was a bad idea to agree to the signing in the first place. I thought I could do it. I thought I had moved on...I'm sorry, Lovie."

"You're selfish," she said, her voice a low growl.

"I know," Saxon replied, sighing. "I know."

"You are so damn selfish. You got everything you wanted. God, I'm so stupid." She pointed at him. "I had a feeling you were going to do this."

"Do what?" Saxon asked, taken aback. He had never seen Lovie so angry. She was right; he had been selfish and he knew it. But what choice did he have? He didn't want to deal with Sloane again; she hadn't changed a bit.

Lovie glared at him. "You know what. You'll be fine, Mr. Wall Street, won't you? Meanwhile, I was counting on that money. I am supporting my sister and my nieces right now and I can't do that without this tour. But that's not your problem, right? Fuck the tall, dark girl, she'll fall into my bed easily."

Saxon frowned. "That's not what this is, Lovie. You know that."

He was at a loss.

Lovie paced back and forth, her arms folded tightly across her chest, and he could see that she was livid. "I don't know anything. All I know is that you let an insensitive, possessive asshole get under your skin cause he's fucking your ex-wife, who clearly still has feelings for you. I don't know how I got sucked into the middle of this dumpster fire."

Lovie pulled her phone from her purse and began stabbing the screen.

He sighed. "I'll take you back to your hotel."

"No, don't bother. We're done. I'll catch a taxi or whatever I can get in this fucking small backwater, out-in-the-middle-of-fucking-nowhere town! God, I'm an idiot."

"Let me take you back." Saxon said, approaching her. "We can talk about this."

Lovie shook her head. "Unless you're going to tell me we're still on for the signing, I have nothing to say to you." Her voice was softer but he heard the determination in it and knew she was done.

He watched her turn and head back into the restaurant, presumably to have them call a car for her.

Saxon felt like the lowest creature on the planet. He groaned in frustration. He knew this dinner was a bad idea.

He couldn't do the signing. Sloane had manipulated him for the last time and he needed to be done.

The next morning, Saxon called Sloane's publisher and canceled the book signing. They tried to dissuade him but he stood firm.

As the day wore on, the weight of his decision started to sink in. He had let Lovie down in the worst way possible. She had been counting on him, and he had failed her. Saxon couldn't stop thinking about her, even as he worked in the store. But he couldn't bring himself to face her yet.

Saxon walked around the store, straightening shelves and checking inventory, thinking about how he might fix things with Lovie. He looked up when he heard the door chime and a familiar figure sauntered toward him.

Sloane looked as stunning as ever and Saxon's mood darkened. His world was falling to pieces while Sloane was having the time of her life.

"What are you doing here?" Saxon asked, trying to keep the irritation out of his voice.

"I heard the signing was canceled." Sloane replied, her voice silky smooth. "I just wanted to make sure you were okay."

"I'm fine," Saxon said shortly. "You can go now."

Sloane glanced at the door then moved in closer, her hips

swaying. "Saxon, I was hoping you'd comply, but now, I'm going to have to do things the hard way."

Sloane smiled and stepped even closer, her body almost touching his. Saxon resisted the urge to step back.

"Once upon a time, you would have done anything for me," she said, her voice as smooth as honey. "But I suppose those days are long gone."

Saxon took a deep breath. He remembered all too well. He had loved Sloane once—or thought he did—but that was a long time ago.

Saxon sighed. "What do you want, Sloane?"

"I told Tarik about the bookstore deal in confidence. I didn't expect him to blab it to you the moment he had a chance."

"What are you talking about?" Saxon asked.

"Remember how quickly the old geezer, what was his name? Cyrus Mohr? Remember how quickly he signed over the store? That was all my doing."

Saxon glanced at her in horror. "What are you saying? What did you do?"

Sloane smiled. "I took care of him. I made sure he signed over the store to you, no questions asked. I guess he was tired of running the place anyway."

"What did you do?" Saxon repeated, his voice rising. "What did you do to Mr. Mohr?"

"All you need to know is that I convinced him to sell you the store. You got a good deal and he got paid. Everyone's happy." She wiped her hands together like there was dust on them.

Saxon couldn't believe what he was hearing.

"Hang on a second." he said. "You need to tell me exactly what you did."

"Just forget it, Saxon. Back then I really thought you deserved the store. You loved it; it's your dream. But if you're going to be a sore loser and cancel the signing, then I guess there's nothing more to talk about."

"Just tell me what you did." Saxon repeated, his voice low and dark.She acted like she hadn't heard him.

"Now, what happened with Lovie? I'm surprised she's not here." Sloane looked around. "Oh wait, she's probably pissed that you canceled. She needed this gig, you know."

Saxon's fists clenched at the mention of Lovie. He couldn't believe Sloane had the audacity to bring her up after everything that had happened. "Just tell me what you did to Mr. Mohr," he growled.

Sloane didn't flinch. Instead, she smirked. "Oh, Saxon. You're so predictable. You always did have a temper. It's one of the things I loved about you."

Saxon took another step away from her, needing to keep his distance as his anger grew. "Tell me what you did, Sloane," he repeated, his voice low and dangerous.

Sloane's smirk faded slightly, but she still didn't back down. "I don't see why it matters now," she said, her voice laced with annoyance. "The store is yours, fair and square. You should be thanking me."

"I will not thank you for whatever underhanded thing you did to get me this store."

Saxon's voice was cold and hard. He took a step towards Sloane, towering over her. Sloane, for her part, didn't back down. She met his gaze, her eyes icy and unflinching.

"You don't know what you're getting into, Saxon," she said, her voice a low whisper. "You have no idea what kind of world you're entering. But if you want to know what I did, fine. I'll tell you."

Saxon waited, his fists clenched, as Sloane continued to speak.

"I found out that Cyrus had secrets he desperately wanted to keep hidden so I reassured him they'd stay buried, as long as he let the store go. Like I said, everyone's happy."

"So why tell Tarik those lies?" Saxon wanted to know. "Why tell him I took advantage of Cyrus?"

She shrugged. "I couldn't very well tell him the truth, could

I?" She ran a hand over a display of coffee table books. "Or maybe I could. There's some hood in Tarik that I find intriguing. Like he could have easily gone into a life of crime had things gone a different way. I don't know...anyway, I think he's a little obsessed with you. He thinks you did me wrong."

Saxon ran a hand over her face. He needed to get Sloane out of his store before he lost it. "Are you done with your little evil reveal?"

"Yep, I need to get going." She looked around the store, seemingly taking it all in for the first time. "I must admit, when you told me you wanted to open a bookstore, I was thinking of a crappy little store tucked inside a crappy strip mall but you've outdone yourself...top shelf Kentucky bourbon, a media room, probably the nicest bookstore I've ever seen."

Saxon nodded, opening the door for her.

"I'm sure you'll do well here. I'll swing by in a couple of days." And then she was gone.

Sloane's visit unnerved Saxon. The thought of her and Tarik plotting against him all this time was infuriating.

He knew Sloane was planning something and he had a sneaking suspicion that Tarik knew more than he was letting on, but he had no proof. He'd have to figure this out on his own.

Saxon felt a pang of guilt and regret. He hadn't meant to let Sloane affect him this way and he never should have agreed to the book signing in the first place. He should have told Lovie how he was feeling sooner, but now it was too late.

He called Lovie but her phone went immediately to voicemail. At least she hadn't blocked him. "I'm sorry, Lovie," Saxon said finally. "I'm so sorry for not telling you how I feel sooner. It's been so hard for me, being around her again after all these years. It brings up a lot of old feelings and I didn't know how to deal with them."

He paused, trying to make his words make sense. "But that's no excuse," he continued, forcing himself to be honest. "I let her get under my skin and it caused me to make bad decisions."

Saxon took a deep breath. "I want to see your face when I ask for forgiveness so I'll save that for then and pray that you will eventually allow me to see you again."

He ended the call and placed the phone on the table. She had no reason to call him back.

Why would Lovie ever forgive him? She'd gotten caught up in the messy relationship that Saxon and Sloane had created and if he was being fair, Sloane hadn't been the only one at fault. He had neglected her while he'd grown his business and he'd never really asked her if she wanted to own a bookstore. He'd just assumed his dream was her dream.

Sighing, Saxon locked the store up for the night and dragged himself up the stairs to his bed.

A few nights later, he was dreaming of Lovie when he woke with a start. He frowned, unsure if he was still dreaming and trying to piece together what happened. He and Lovie were sitting in the media room and he'd grabbed her hand, told her he loved her but she'd yanked her hand away in horror. She'd thrown a bottle of wine at him, calling him a liar and he'd woken right before the bottle could make contact with his temple.

Saxon ran a hand over his face. His skin was damp with sweat and he sat up in bed, the chill in the air causing goosebumps on his exposed skin.

The apartment was dark; the time on his bedside clock read a few minutes after three in the morning.

As he sat there, trying to calm his mind, Saxon heard a strange noise coming from below. It sounded like someone was trying to break in. He sat up straighter, listening intently. He realized that he had been so wrapped up in his own misery that he had forgotten to set the alarm. And he'd left his phone downstairs.

Saxon cursed, then quickly got out of bed and grabbed a baseball bat from his closet. He crept down the stairs, his heart pounding in his chest as he tried to remain as quiet as possible. He could hear the intruder moving around, knocking things over and rummaging through the shelves.

Saxon gripped the bat tighter in his hand as he reached the bottom of the stairs. He took a deep breath and peeked around the corner, trying to get a glimpse of the intruder.

Pain shot through the back of his head as he crumpled to the floor.

When Saxon woke up, he was lying at the foot of the stairs. His head was pounding and his vision was blurry. He wondered how long he'd been unconscious.

As his senses slowly came back to him, he realized that the intruder was still there. He could hear the sound of footsteps coming closer to him.

He tried to sit up but his whole body ached. He could feel the cold, hard floor beneath him and he shivered. He knew he had to defend himself.

Slowly, he raised the baseball bat, ready to strike. But before he could make a move, he heard a familiar voice.

"Saxon, man, you all right?" Robbie Boyd, the town sheriff asked, bending down.

No, he wasn't all right. Everything hurt, including his heart. "I don't know...store robbed." he managed to say.

Robbie helped Saxon to his feet and guided him to a chair. Saxon winced as he sat down. The room was spinning and he felt like he was about to pass out again.

Robbie took out his notepad and pen. "Did you see who did this?"

Saxon shook his head, his hand grazed the back of his head where he'd been hit and he winced. The wound was too tender to touch. "No, I heard someone breaking in and went downstairs. I tried to defend myself but they hit me from behind."

Robbie frowned, concerned. "Looks like you took a pretty hard hit to the head. I've got an ambulance on the way to get you checked out."

Robbie scribbled in his notepad, "I'm going to need to take a statement from you, Saxon. And we'll need to look at the security footage to see if we can identify the intruder."

Saxon's gaze fell on his bourbon bar. There was a glass case that contained several bottles of high end collector versions of Kentucky bourbon, including a rare bottle of Pappy Van Winkle he'd gotten as a store opening gift from his uncle. That bottle alone was worth five figures due to its age and rarity. The glass was shattered and the shelves were empty.

Saxon felt a wave of anger wash over him. This store was his life's work and someone had violated it in the worst way possible. The thought of someone stealing his precious collection of bourbons made his blood boil.

Saxon's mind raced with suspicion. Every instinct told him that Sloane was behind this break-in. He had no concrete evidence, but the more he thought about it, the more obvious it became. Did she really go this far to get what she wanted?

CHAPTER 12

Lovie

Lovie pulled into the garage of her townhouse in Charlotte and cut the engine. She was still fuming; the four-hour drive hadn't come close to calming her outrage.

Saxon had canceled the book signing just because he and Tarik were comparing dicks. That was all there was to it. And Sloane, she could tell, loved the attention.

Lovie banged her head against the steering wheel. She had to get it together before she went inside. Her nieces would be clamoring for Aunt Love's attention, God knew they needed it as they wouldn't get it from their father. He'd divorced the kids along with Layla, which made her anger flare up all over again. Those two girls were the sweetest kids on the planet and they had done nothing wrong.

What the hell was wrong with these men?

She leaned her head back against the headrest. What the hell was wrong with her? She thought Saxon was different. When would she learn not to get her feelings involved? Hw many times would she have to stitch her broken heart back together before she learned. Never mix business with pleasure.

The garage door creaked open and Lovie watched as two small heads peered out. She shook her head. "I'm coming, girls."

Later, after dinner and bath time, Lovie's nieces Jeneva and Jasmine were settled in bed as she told them about Kissing Springs and the festival she'd visited. "Well, Auntie Love, I want to go to a festival when we get there," Jasmine, the youngest, declared.

Lovie smiled down at the little girl. "We can definitely find a festival for us to go to, sweetie." She hugged her nieces close, feeling a sense of warmth spread through her body. This was what she needed right now - the love and innocence of her family.

Layla popped her head in the room. "We've got a busy day tomorrow, tell Auntie Love good night." She eyed Lovie.

Lovie knew that look well. Her sister meant for her to follow her lead and back her up. She stood, then kissed each girl on the forehead. "Good night."

She followed Layla back to the den. Her sister had poured two glasses of red wine and placed them on the coffee table. Lovie sighed as she took a sip and the warmth of the alcohol traveled through her. She needed this drink.

Layla sipped from her glass. "You were in the car a while and you looked like you were ready to spit fire. What happened?"

Lovie sighed deeply. She really didn't want to male bash with Layla tonight. Her sister's divorce had understandably left her less than happy with the whole male gender. "The book tour has been canceled. The whole thing was a bad idea from the start."

She told her sister about the disastrous dinner and Saxon's decision to cancel.

Layla leaned back on the couch. "I hate to say I told you so but," she shrugged. "What happens with you and Saxon now?"

She had no idea. "I told him we were done. So I guess nothing." The thought burned her gut more than the wine. She hated to admit it but she missed him already.

"Are you sure you still want to go back there for the week? Maybe we should go to the beach instead," Layla asked, picking up her wine glass again. "I have to give it to you, your taste in wine is impeccable."

"Thanks, but we're getting the place for less than the cost of a hotel room for a night. We might as well go. I think the trip will do us all some good."

"What are you going to do now that the signing isn't happening?" Layla asked.

"We will be filming more footage of the golf course, so pack your best golf gear." And trying her best not to think about the look on Saxon's face when she'd told him they were done.

The golf course project was coming along and Stan had asked for some additional marketing videos so she had plenty of work for the week.

Layla nodded. "Anytime I think of golf gear, I picture plaid and those hats with the pompoms on them. Not really my style."

"Yeah, no, the sport has come a long way since then. I was thinking of creating some shirts with my logo on them that we can wear."

"That's a great idea! I can work on that." She paused. "How are you really? And what happens when you run into Saxon again?"

Her heart thudded at the sound of his name. "Don't know. I can't focus on any of that right now."

Layla grabbed her hand. "I'm the last person you'd expect to say this but maybe you should think about things from his standpoint."

Lovie gaped at her sister. She'd been bashing her ex and the whole male species for months and now she was asking Lovie to have empathy?

"I know, I know, but divorce is rough. It makes people do stupid things...or undo the stupid things they did when they were in love. He's probably trying to protect his peace." Layla nudged her. "Not saying you should forgive him but at least try to see his side of things."

Lovie considered her sister's words. Maybe she was being too harsh on Saxon. Maybe he was just trying to avoid any unnecessary drama. She took another sip of her wine and drummed her fingers on the table. "Maybe you're right. I shouldn't be so quick to judge."

Layla grinned. "I expected way more resistance from you."

Lovie rolled her eyes but smiled back.

"I'm not always as stubborn as you make me out to be." It was good to have her sister by her side again. They'd always been there for each other, even during the darkest of times. "Thanks for being here, Layla. I don't know what I'd do without you."

Layla squeezed her hand. "You've been a Godsend for me and the girls. I know it's a lot to take in three people into your space but I appreciate you for doing it. The least I can do is offer you some sisterly advice." They clinked their glasses together before settling into a comfortable silence.

Swirling her wine glass, Layla said, "I was kinda hoping to meet this renaissance man of yours before you called it quits, though. I mean, come on, you found a man that loves books more than you do."

Lovie thought of the bookworm tucked in her purse and wanted to cry. But she wouldn't break down in front of her sister. She slurped the last of the wine. "Yeah, I figured he was too good to be true. That's what I get for trying."

The morning they were to leave for their trip to Kissing Springs, Lovie woke early with a sense of calm. As she showered and prepared for the day, she considered her sister's advice. Maybe it wasn't fair to be so quick to judge Saxon. She'd convinced him to do the signing even though he'd made it clear he wanted nothing to do with his ex-wife any longer and things had gone south before the signing could even happen.

A scratching outside her door followed by a soft thud got her attention.

"Ouch! Stop, Mommy said to be quiet!"

"I am being quiet!" came the not so quiet reply.

Lovie chuckled and quickly finished dressing. She knew if she didn't intervene fast, one or both girls would be crying and trying to convince her of the other's sins.

She opened her bedroom door to find both girls camped on the hardwood floor like they'd spent hours waiting for her to wake up. "Good morning ladies! Let's go make breakfast so we can get on the road."

Jasmine and Jeneva cheered, each trying to be the first to give her a hug. Lovie smiled as she hugged them both. "We are going to have so much fun today!"

They made their way to the kitchen where Lovie started to prepare breakfast while the girls helped by setting the table. Lovie felt grateful for the busy morning, it kept her mind off Saxon and the cancelled book signing.

Layla appeared, placing the girls' bags near the door. "I want clean plates. The sooner you eat, the sooner we can hit the road. Jeneva, no more pepper! Your eggs are going to be too spicy."

Lovie placed a mug of coffee in her sister's hand.

As the four of them ate breakfast, Lovie made a mental checklist of everything she needed to do before they left since they would be gone for a week.

"I'll drive first, I know there's probably work you need to catch up on."

After breakfast, they loaded up the car and started their journey to Kissing Springs. The drive was fairly peaceful. Jasmine napped most of the way and Jeneva played with her tablet.

When they arrived at the house, Lovie was pleasantly surprised. The house was bigger than she expected with a play area for the kids downstairs and a spacious living room. Layla and the girls ran around the house, admiring everything. Lovie checked out each bedroom and in the last one, called out to the girls.

They gasped when they entered the room. There was a large mural of rainbow colored horses and butterflies on the wall opposite a white bunk bed with stairs leading to the top bunk. There were children's books and toys on a white shelving unit and a whole case of board games. "We can have Game Nite!" Jeneva gasped.

Lovie nodded. "Yes we can."

Layla had the girls unpack and put their things away as Lovie found a bedroom with a desk that she could use for her work. She set her laptop and portable monitor up and responded to her email. A small part of her, the part that loved romance, longed to know how Saxon was and wondered why he hadn't at least attempted to reach out.

Why would he? She told him it was over; She'd called him selfish and basically pushed him back into his ex-wife's arms.

She sighed, realizing she wasn't going to get much work done thinking about Saxon, then got up from the desk to check on the girls.

As she walked down the stairs, she heard Layla giggling with the girls. Lovie smiled at the sound. It had been a while since she heard her sister so carefree. The girls were trying on fairy wings and casting spells on each other.

"So what's on the agenda for the rest of the day?" Lovie asked.

"We need groceries." Layla glanced at the girls. "But we're playing and I don't think we all need to go to the store. Girls, I'll be right back. Finish getting your princess outfits on and we'll take pictures."

Layla rose and motioned to Lovie to follow.

"Let's make a list of stuff we need and you can sneak out to the store while I do the photo shoot."

"Why am I sneaking off to the store?" Lovie asked.

"Because you don't want two children begging for random crap every aisle you go down." She pulled open drawers until she found a small notebook and a pen. "Trust me on this."

~

Lovie was marveling at the high cost of children's cereal when she heard a voice behind her.

"Lovie Whitfield does her own grocery shopping? Who knew?" The voice was deep and familiar. Lovie turned around to see Tarik, Sloane's boyfriend, standing a few feet away from her

She glanced around, assuming Sloane was close by.

"Yeah, imagine that. How are you?"

"Can't complain. So," he gave her a slow once over. "Are you in town for a while? I still want to talk to you about doing some marketing for my business. Maybe over dinner?"

"I don't think that's a good idea, especially after our last dinner together."

"This would just be the two of us. I'd love to hear your ideas, get to know you a little better," he said, his meaning clear.

Lovie resisted the urge to recoil but the thought made her cringe inside. "Why don't you call my office first thing tomorrow and we can talk about a marketing plan?"

Tarik's mood changed immediately. "Oh, I get it. You only have time for men with money? Or is it that you only like half breeds like Saxon? I'm not light skinned enough for you?"

"I never said anything like that. And I'm not interested in a man's money."

He snorted. "Sure you aren't. Women are always interested in a man with deep pockets." Tarik crossed his arms over his massive chest. "But Saxon's pockets might not be as deep as you think. His store got robbed the other night and I heard they got away with his prized bourbon collection."

Lovie raised a hand to her mouth. "That's awful. Is he okay?"

"He got roughed up a bit but he'll live," Tarik said, his tone almost casual. "Too bad his security system wasn't as good as his bourbon collection."

Lovie narrowed her eyes. There was something in the way Tarik said that last part that made her suspicious. "What are you saying, Tarik?"

He shrugged. "Just that there are some things you can't protect. And sometimes, things go missing for a reason."

"What reason would that be?"

Tarik leaned in closer to her, his voice low. "Maybe someone wanted to get their hands on that collection real bad. Or maybe they wanted to send a message to Saxon."

"What message?"

Tarik grinned. "That's not for me to say. But if I were you, I'd keep my distance from him and that store for a while."

Lovie felt a chill run down her spine. Tarik's words were ominous, and the way he said them made her wonder if he had anything to do with the robbery and assault. It wasn't like her to jump to conclusions, but she couldn't shake the feeling that something was off. "Thanks for the warning, Tarik. I'll keep that in mind."

He smirked. "Always looking out for you, Lovie. See you around."

As he walked away, Lovie couldn't help but watch him with suspicion. There was something about him that made her uneasy. She finished grabbing her groceries and made her way back to the house, her mind racing with thoughts of Saxon and what Tarik had said.

After putting the groceries away, Lovie told the girls and Layla that she needed to make a quick phone call.

CHAPTER 13
Saxon

Saxon paced around the living room of his Uncle Charlie's house, desperate for answers. Uncle Charlie and his cousin Jameson sat in the armchairs on either side of the fireplace, trying to reason with him.

"Saxon, stop pacing and sit down," Uncle Charlie said, with a heavy sigh. "You're wearing out my carpet."

Saxon stopped in his tracks, his face grim. "I can't believe this happened," he said, shaking his head. "Someone broke into my store and took my bourbon."

Uncle Charlie's voice was firm. "We don't know what happened yet, Saxon. But I promise you, we will find out. Now, have a seat. Let's go over the facts one more time and see if we can make sense of it all. Who would do something like this?"

Saxon rubbed his temple, then reluctantly took a seat on the sofa. "I don't know. I went downstairs because I heard a noise then next thing I know, I got knocked upside the head. That's what I'm trying to figure out. It could be anyone."

Jameson crossed his arms. "Seems kind of suspicious that it happened the day you were supposed to host Sloane's book signing, doesn't it?"

Saxon felt a chill run through him at the words. "You think

Sloane was behind this?" He couldn't believe that his ex-wife could do something like this. It didn't make any sense.

Uncle Charlie tented his fingers. "Let's not jump to conclusions," he said gently. "We don't know what happened here yet."

"I wouldn't put it past her," Jameson's lips formed a thin line. "And didn't you tell us she's dating a new man?"

Saxon's jaw clenched. He got bad vibes from Tarik but theft?

A thought occurred to him. When Sloane had stopped by, he caught her eyeing the bourbon collection on more than one occasion. Had she been casing his bookstore?

Saxon's mind raced with suspicion and anger. "I can't believe this," he muttered. "Tarik might have something to do with it, too."

"Tarik?" Uncle Charlie raised an eyebrow.

"He's Sloane's new man," Saxon explained.

Jameson looked up. "That's him? You know what, I met him. He stopped by the gym last week. Wanted to know if I had any construction needs. He gave me former inmate vibes."

Uncle Charlie stroked his chin, lost in thought. "Well, we can't jump to conclusions. We need to gather more information first."

Saxon nodded, his mind still racing. His gut told him that Tarik was involved. Maybe he was just being paranoid, but something about the man didn't sit right with him. He needed to find out more about him, and fast.

"I'll look into Tarik," Saxon said, determination in his voice. "But in the meantime, I need to figure out how to get my bourbon back."

Uncle Charlie stood and put a hand on Saxon's shoulder. "We'll help you, son. Jameson and I will do whatever it takes to get your stolen goods back."

Saxon felt a sense of relief wash over him. He couldn't do this alone. "Thanks, Uncle. I appreciate it."

"Let's start by checking the security footage from your store," Jameson suggested. "Maybe we can get a lead on who did this."

Saxon nodded in agreement. "Good idea. Let's head over there now."

When they arrived at the store, Saxon led them into the media room. He pulled up the footage from the night of the break-in and started scanning through it as Jameson and Uncle Charlie watched.

Two shadowy figures appeared on the camera, both with ski caps covering their faces.

Saxon's heart raced as he watched the footage. The two figures moved swiftly, their movements calculated and precise. They went straight for the locked cabinet where Saxon's most valuable bourbon bottles were kept. With ease, they broke it open and started filling their bags with Saxon's prized collection.

Before they could empty the cabinet, they stopped and turned in the direction of the stairs.

"They must have heard me walking around upstairs," Saxon murmured. The spot where he'd been struck throbbed. One man tilted his head as if telling the other to go check it out. The other man set his bag down, pulled a small object from his pocket, then swiftly strode toward the stairs.

"What's that in his hand?" Uncle Charlie peered at the screen.

Saxon zoomed in on the footage, trying to get a clearer view of what the man was holding. It looked like a smaller version of a police baton, and Saxon knew what was coming next.

He watched in horror as the man waited at the base of the stairs, just out of Saxon's view, weapon in hand. Saxon winced as he saw himself, bat in hand, move cautiously down the stairs. As soon as he reached the bottom stair, without hesitation, the man stepped out from his hiding spot and swung the baton at Saxon's head, hitting him with a sickening thud.

Jameson swore as they watched Saxon fall to the ground, unconscious. The men quickly grabbed the rest of the bottles and ran out of the store.

When the footage ended, Saxon sat back in his chair, his head throbbing. "All of this took less than ten minutes, so they planned the robbery carefully."

"Do you recognize either of them?" Uncle Charlie asked.

Saxon paused the video where both men were visible. "One of them could be Tarik but I'm not one hundred percent sure." He pointed at the figure he thought could be Tarik. "That one."

"You need to get a copy of this video over to Sheriff Boyd," Jameson said.

"Already done." Saxon closed his laptop and looked at his uncle and cousin. "I'm going to Louisville. Sloane knows something and I'm going to get some answers out of her then I'll deal with Tarik."

"Not a good idea, Saxon," his uncle protested. "Let the authorities handle this. You don't know what kind of man Tarik is or what he's capable of."

Saxon shook his head. "I have to go. I have a lead on Tarik, and I need to follow it. I can't just sit here and wait for the sheriff."

Uncle Charlie sighed. "Fine, but be careful." He turned to Jameson. "You go with him, make sure he doesn't do anything rash."

Saxon rose, grateful for the backup. "I will. Thanks, Uncle."

As Saxon and Jameson left the store, Jameson pointed toward his SUV. "I'll drive," he said. "You can navigate. Where are we going in Louisville?"

"Her house. The rental property she got from the divorce settlement."

As they drove to Louisville, Saxon tried to stay calm even though he wanted to punch something. How could Sloane have been involved in this? Was this her way of paying him back for canceling the book signing?

When they arrived at Sloane's house, Saxon's heart was pounding in his chest. He was determined to find out the truth no matter what it took. He knocked on the door with purpose, ready to confront Sloane about the break-in.

The door swung open, revealing Sloane standing there with a smug expression on her face. "Well, well, well. The Mitchell men decided to pay me a visit," she said slyly.

Saxon's jaw clenched. "You know why I'm here." He pushed his way past her and into the house, Jameson close behind him.

Sloane shrugged. "Do I? Enlighten me."

"Don't play dumb, Sloane. I know you had something to do with the break-in at my store."

Sloane rolled her eyes. "Again with that damn store. Why are you questioning me?"

Saxon watched her closely. "Because you're involved with Tarik, and he's the one who did it. I saw the footage, and I saw him there."

Sloane's expression faltered for a moment before she regained her composure. "I don't know what you're talking about. And even if I did, why would I help Tarik steal your bourbon? What would be in it for me?"

Saxon stepped closer to her, his eyes narrowing. "How did you know the bourbon was taken?"

Sloane's eyes flashed in anger. "How dare you storm into my house accusing me of theft...you're the one who picked that damn store over me, remember?"

Clarity struck him at that moment. This wasn't about the bourbon at all. "Sloane," he said, "the robbery was all your idea, wasn't it?"

Sloane glared at him in response, her face a mix of rage and hatred. "Maybe it was, and maybe it wasn't," she said defiantly.

Saxon shook his head. He didn't need her to confirm it; he already knew the answer. "It's over, Sloane," he said softly. "You're not going to get away with this. I'll make sure of it."

"Let's go, Jay." He motioned to Jameson then turned to leave but Sloane's voice behind him made him pause.

"I told them to burn it down, you know."

"What did you say?" he whipped around to face Sloane.

She wouldn't meet his eyes. "I said that if you weren't in the store, they could set the damn thing on fire. So you could feel what it's like to have something you love taken from you."

That's why the break-in had seemed so personal. They hadn't been after the bourbon; they'd been after revenge. Saxon clenched his fists in fury. "Why would you do that? You almost cost me my life!"

Sloane shook her head. "You weren't supposed to be home. I assumed you'd be out with the publicist. I didn't say anything about harming you."

Like that made things better. "Where is Tarik?"

She shrugged. "No idea. We've parted ways."

"I don't believe you. Where is he?" Saxon demanded.

"Hell if I know. Maybe back in Kissing Springs."

Saxon closed his eyes, tried counting to ten before he did something rash. Opening his eyes, he moved closer to Sloane. "If you hear from Tarik, you let me know immediately. And you tell him I'm coming for him."

Sloane crossed her arms, looking bored with the whole affair. "I don't expect I'll hear from him. He got the booze and I got what I needed from him so what he does now isn't my concern."

Saxon couldn't believe he'd been married to this woman. He'd planned to spend the rest of his life with her when they took their vows. Now he realized he didn't know her at all.

He shook his head. "Jay, let's get out of here."

Jameson followed as he stormed out of the house, his blood boiling.

They got back in the car and drove off without another word, Saxon's mind racing.

Jameson finally spoke once they were on the highway. "Aren't you glad you're not married to that train wreck anymore?"

"Hell, it feels like I still am. I thought I was done with her drama but clearly I was wrong." Saxon ran a hand over his face. "Lovie's gone, my store is damaged and I can't even drink my sorrows away because that fucking thick neck thug stole my good bourbon."

"Wait, what happened with Lovie?" Jameson took his eyes off the road briefly to gawk at Saxon.

"I canceled the book signing and Lovie lost the gig," Saxon admitted wearily. "She thinks Sloane has done all of this because she wants me back. She said we're done."

"Ok...and you're just going to let her go?"

This was why he hadn't told anyone in his family about the Lovie situation. He knew they'd give him shit about it. "No," he said, crossing his arms. "I've got a plan."

Jameson snorted. "Oh yeah? And what's your plan?"

"I've been asking around at the small business events to see who needs a PR rep. I'm trying to find her gigs. Unfortunately, no one, well, besides Stan, needs her services."

"Well, I'll enlighten you. Stan is trying to keep her to himself. He found out the book signing was canceled and he's hired her on for more work and telling everyone she's booked."

Saxon's mouth dropped and he stared at his cousin. "What the hell? How did you hear all this?"

"The monthly Small Business Society meetings I've been trying to get you to come to. But yeah, I'm surprised you didn't know. Anyway, you need to come up with another plan to win her back. Seems like she's got the job thing covered," Jameson said. "You know she's in town this week, right?"

He nodded. He knew this was the week she was bringing her sister and nieces to stay in Kissing Springs, and he'd hoped she'd stop by to see him but that was wistful thinking on his part.

"You gotta do the grand gesture, man. I had to do it for Noemie. And my grand gesture, if I say so myself, was irresistible. Noemie couldn't help but fall all the way into my arms."

Saxon's eyes rolled. Jameson was always boasting about his grand gesture when his wife wasn't within earshot. He knew better.

Jameson continued. "You need to let Lovie know she can trust and hopefully can't live without you. You play your cards right and see if you can convince her to move here. We like her and think she'll be good for you."

They pulled up in front of the boarded-up bookstore.

Saxon paused before getting out of Jameson's vehicle. "Any ideas since you're the self-proclaimed grand gesture king?"

"Show her you've been listening and you hear her, understand her." Jameson gave his arm a quick slug. "You're the smart one in the family, you'll come up with something."

Saxon sighed. "Man...I don't know."

Jameson's expression softened. "You can do it. Good luck. We're rooting for you."

After Jameson left, Saxon made his way up to his apartment, turning his cousin's words around in his head.

Grand gesture? What could he do for Lovie that she couldn't do for herself? Thanks to his business and his former career on Wall Street, he lived a very comfortable life. He could help Lovie financially, but she'd see his help as charity.

What could he do to show her that he wanted her by his side?

CHAPTER 14
Lovie

On the drive back to the vacation house, Lovie considered Tarik's words, analyzing his tone and body language. The more she thought about it, the more it seemed like he was threatening Saxon.

But maybe she was making more of the situation than she needed to? Was that possible?

Lovie had to admit she still had strong feelings for Saxon. Yes, she was still furious that he'd canceled Sloane's signing but the more she thought about it, she might have done the same thing in his position.

Was Sloane as petty as Saxon made her out to be? The woman had everything going for her: she was beautiful, men seemed to fall at her feet, now she was a best-selling author. Was it possible that she'd gotten Tarik to break into The Book Barrel and steal Saxon's collection? Or had he done the deed on his own?

She needed to find answers and quickly.

Debating whether what she was about to do was a good idea, she pulled over into a vacant shopping center lot and turned off the car.

Lovie dug into her purse. if she found the card on the first try, she'd call. If not, then she'd come up with another plan.

She pulled Tarik's card from the bottom of her bag along with a perfume sample stick and an old note from Jasmine formally protesting Jeneva's behavior while Lovie was out of town. She put the note aside and scanned the business card.

The card had Tarik's office and cell numbers on it.

What would she say when she called him?

Hey, just checking to make sure you don't plan to harm this man I care about, if it's not too much trouble?

Lovie sighed, realizing how ridiculous that sounded. But she had to do something to ease her mind.

She needed to play it cool, maybe flirt a little, and see what information she could gather. She knew from experience that sometimes people gave away more than they intended when they felt comfortable.

Taking a deep breath, Lovie dialed Tarik's cell number. It rang twice before he answered.

"What's up, Lovie?" Tarik's voice was smooth and confident.

Lovie forced herself to calm down and focus on her plan. "Hey, Tarik. I wanted to talk to you about real estate investing... Sloane mentioned you might be taking on beginners? Maybe you and I could grab dinner sometime?"

There was a pause on the other end of the line, and Lovie wondered if she had made a mistake. But then Tarik chuckled. "I knew you'd come around. How about tonight? We can go to the Boot Scoot."

Lovie's heart raced. She hadn't expected him to say yes so quickly. "That sounds great. How about I meet you there?"

Tarik agreed, and they hung up. Lovie took a deep breath and started her car. She had no idea what she was getting herself into, but she was determined to find out the truth about Tarik's involvement in the robbery.

Later, after changing quickly into a bar appropriate black dress and heels, and ducking out of the vacation house before Layla and the girls caught her, Lovie parked her car in front of the Boot Scoot. She realized how nervous she was. She was going to be alone with someone she suspected of being involved in a crime. What if Tarik turned on her? Could she defend herself? She hadn't thought about bringing a weapon; the pepper spray she kept on hand was at home in her other purse.

She hit the steering wheel in frustration. She'd have to wing it if needed.

She sent her sister a quick text.

> If I call or text you and I say something about Mom, treat it like an SOS and call 911. I'm heading to the Boot Scoot bar.

Layla's reply was quick.

> Should I even ask what you're up to?

> No. I'll call you later.

When Tarik pulled up a few minutes later, Lovie stepped out of her car and greeted him with a smile. His face lit up when he saw her, and the two of them made their way into the bar.

The restaurant was bustling with loud music playing and people laughing and talking. Tarik led them to a table near the back.

They talked about small things as they ate dinner, mostly about Tarik's favorite subject: Tarik.

But then, the conversation turned to Saxon and the stolen bourbon. Lovie played it cool, asking Tarik if he knew anything more about the theft.

Tarik's demeanor changed in an instant. He grew tense and guarded, refusing to say anything further on the matter. Lovie knew she had hit a nerve.

As dinner ended, Lovie excused herself to the restroom, trying to come up with a new plan. It was clear that Tarik wasn't going to give away any information willingly.

As she walked back to the table, she squared her shoulders. She'd have to ratchet things up a notch.

"So where is Sloane? Surely she didn't just let you loose tonight," Lovie said, her voice lowered and sexy.

Tarik snorted. "You don't need to worry about her."

Lovie paused. What exactly did that mean? "Oh? Why not? Her leash on you seemed pretty tight."

He chuckled, baring his teeth. "Nah, your boy Saxon might play that shit but I don't. No one controls me."

She saw her opportunity. "He's not mine. We're done."

Tarik raised a brow. "Oh so that's why you're sniffing around me, huh?"

Lovie leaned in, placing her hand on Tarik's thigh. "Maybe. Or maybe I just find you incredibly attractive."

Tarik's eyes flickered with desire, and Lovie knew she had him. "And what do you want from me?" he asked, his voice low and husky.

"I want to know the truth," Lovie said, her lips inches away from Tarik's. "Did you steal that bourbon?"

Tarik's expression turned cold, but Lovie didn't falter. "And if I did?" he asked.

"Then I want you to confess," Lovie said, her hand trailing up Tarik's thigh. "I want to know everything."

Tarik leaned back in his chair, his eyes never leaving Lovie's face. "What if I don't want to confess?" he asked, a hint of challenge in his voice.

Lovie leaned in closer, her lips almost touching Tarik's ear. "Then I'll have to find another way to make you talk," she whispered, her hand now on his chest.

Tarik's breathing grew shallow, and Lovie knew she had him right where she wanted him. She stood up from the table, extending her hand to him. "Let's go back to your place," she said, her voice sultry. "I'll make it worth your while."

Tarik didn't say anything, but he grabbed Lovie's hand and followed her out of the restaurant. Lovie's heart was racing as they made their way to her car. She knew she was playing a dangerous game, but she was determined to get the truth out of Tarik.

As they approached Tarik's car, Lovie heard a voice behind her.

"Lovie? Is that you?" a male voice asked. Jameson, Saxon's cousin, and his wife approached the car. Lovie wanted to fade into the night air.

Her heart sank as she heard Jameson's voice. She quickly let go of Tarik's hand and turned to face them, putting on her best fake smile. "Jameson, nice to see you again."

"What are you doing here with this fool?" Jameson asked.

He turned to Tarik. "I know you broke into my cousin's store. Sloane told us everything. You're gonna pay for what you did, one way or another."

Tarik's eyes narrowed at the mention of Sloane's name. His lips curled into a snarl. "I have no idea what you're talking about. And last I checked, you aren't law enforcement so you can cut the threats." Tarik puffed up, getting in Jameson's face.

Jameson made a move toward him, but Noemie placed a hand on his chest. "Jameson, let's go."

Lovie stepped back as Jameson whirled to face her. "Are you seeing this thug behind Saxon's back?"

She wanted to confess her plan but she couldn't break character now.

Lovie squared her shoulders, refusing to back down. "That's none of your business."

"It is my business when he's involved in stealing from my family. You better watch yourself, Lovie. You don't want to get caught up in this mess." Jameson's voice was low and threatening. "We Mitchells take care of our own. You don't want to make enemies out of us."

He took his wife's arm and led her towards the entrance to the bar.

Lovie watched them walk away. Now what? She figured Jameson wouldn't wait to call Saxon and tell him he'd run into her. And would he show up here? The bar was maybe a ten minute drive from the bookstore. She'd had enough drama for the evening; she didn't want to have to explain things to Saxon too.

"That whole fucking family needs to be taught a lesson," Tarik muttered. "Too bad they won't all be in one place."

Lovie turned to him. "What does that mean?"

He studied her and Lovie fought the urge to cross her arms over her chest.

"I don't know what kind of games you're playing, but I'd stay clear of that bookstore for the next few days." He strode to the driver's seat of his car. "Don't say I didn't warn you."

As she watched Tarik's sports car peal out of the parking lot, she realized she'd just been warned-or threatened, depending on how one chose to interpret the words-twice in less than ten minutes.

She tapped a foot on the pavement. Should she call him? Maybe she was making more of the situation than she needed to.

Or maybe she should find out where Tarik was headed in such a hurry.

Lovie quickly got into her car and followed Tarik's car from a distance. As he drove through the city, Lovie noticed that Tarik was driving recklessly, swerving between lanes and cutting off other drivers. Despite her fear, she kept following him, determined to find out where he was going.

He stopped a block away from The Book Barrel and cut the lights, pulling into a dark, deserted parking lot. Lovie sped past, not wanting to rouse his suspicions. She saw a sign for a chain drug store ahead and she pulled in, parking her car near the back of the lot. The store was open twenty-four hours and there were a few cars in the lot.

Should she walk back and see what Tarik was up to? Call Saxon and warn him?

Lovie glanced down. She wasn't exactly in night stalker clothes but at least the short dress was black. The heels would have to go though. She popped the truck of her car and dug out a pair of sneakers she'd planned to ship back to the retailer. She was sure the window of time to return them had long since lapsed. The shoes would come in handy tonight.

She pulled a flashlight from her glove compartment and set out toward Saxon's after locking her car.

Lovie's heart was pounding in her chest. She knew she was playing with fire, following Tarik like this, but she couldn't resist the temptation to find out what he was up to.

Lovie ducked out of sight and pressed herself against the wall of the store. If Tarik was still around, she didn't want to be spotted. She peered around the corner into the alley and her heart sank when she saw his car parked next to a large dumpster.

She slowly made her way along the wall until she was close enough to hear Tarik's voice. She crouched down and strained to hear what he was saying.

"Yeah, that bitch told them I did it. So I need you to hit the store tonight. Like now. Then I'm out."

Lovie raised a hand to her mouth.

Tarik continued. "I know, I know, but this shit needs to be done tonight. You heard?"

She could faintly hear the voice on the other end and strained, leaning in further.

Lovie jumped as Tarik hit the steering wheel with force.

"Dude, I don't want to hear shit about your problems. Get your ass over here so we can get this shit done."

She heard the anger in Tarik's voice.

Lovie heard him toss what she assumed was the phone and knew she needed to get out of there immediately.

Lovie got to her feet and began to run back to her car.

Her hands shook as she tried to unlock her car door. When she finally got in, she locked the doors and sat behind the steering wheel, trying to catch her breath.

Why hadn't she thought to record Tarik on the phone? That would be the proof they needed to arrest him.

She needed to warn Saxon. Her hands were shaking so violently she couldn't hold the phone.

Forcing herself to calm down, Lovie used the voice commands to call Saxon. She'd nearly taken his number out of her contact list when she'd told him they were done, but now she was thankful she hadn't had the courage to do it.

The phone rang and rang.

Why wasn't he picking up? Was Saxon ignoring her calls?

She ended the call and immediately called again.

No answer.

Saxon's voicemail started and Lovie murmured along with it. She'd called so many times before meeting him that she knew it by heart.

She sighed. "Saxon, it's me. Please call me when you get this. And stay away from your store."

An incoming call made her stop. She blinked at the display.

Her sister.

Lovie answered immediately. "Layla, is everything ok?"

"I might ask you the same thing...where are you? It's almost two in the morning!"

"I'm fine, I-I can't find Saxon...what if it's too late? Tarik said now and I think he's in danger," she was trying to speak coherently but knew she was failing.

"Slow down. What's going on?"

"Layla, I can't right now, I have to go. I'll call you later."

Lovie ended the call with her sister and attempted to reach Saxon again. She felt a knot of dread in her stomach as the phone continued to ring with no response.

A large boom rang out and Lovie watched in horror as the sky lit up orange and red with flames.

CHAPTER 15

Saxon

Saxon hung up and wanted to toss his phone against the wall. Jameson had given him all the details and told him to meet them at the Boot Scoot. They'd get the truth out of Tarik and he could deal with Lovie.

His gut twisted at that. Why was Lovie out with Tarik?

Because she'd tossed him aside even after he'd tried to explain why he'd canceled the signing.

She hadn't given him a second thought.

And now she was probably letting Tarik do whatever he wanted to her.

That thought had Saxon seeing red.

Yeah, he was going to the Boot Scoot.

Saxon slammed his bedroom door shut, making his way to his closet where his firearm was stored.

He paused, took a deep breath. If he took the weapon, he was escalating this conflict with Tarik to a new, more dangerous level where anything could happen.

Saxon stood in front of the closet, looking at his firearm and feeling a tug of war between his head and heart. On one hand, he wanted to make sure that Tarik wouldn't hurt Lovie. On the other hand, he didn't want to do anything rash that could get him in trouble.

He exhaled. The gun needed to stay in its place.

As Saxon hurried out of his apartment, his fears kicked in. What if Lovie was truly done with him and had moved on?

When he arrived, he parked his SUV and took a deep breath, trying to calm down. He could hear the loud music and laughter coming from the bar, but he couldn't focus on anything except finding Lovie.

Once he was inside, he scanned the crowd. There was no sign of her. He made his way to the patio.

His cousin Jameson's voice stopped him. "Saxon!"

Saxon blinked, bringing the other man into focus as he strode to the booth where Jameson sat with his wife. "Where is she?"

Jameson shook his head. "They left already. I tried to tell you that but your hard head didn't listen. Take a seat."

"What is she doing with Tarik?" Saxon said more to himself than to Jameson and Noemie as he reluctantly sat across from Jameson. Now that he'd confirmed Lovie wasn't in the bar, there wasn't much reason for him to stay.

"Saxon, you don't know what's going on, did you try to call her?" Noemie asked, reaching over and placing a hand on his arm.

Saxon patted his pockets. In his haste to get to the bar, he'd left his phone at home. "Shit!"

He started to ask for Jameson's phone but Jameson crossed his arms. "Look, you can either go back and get your phone or you can have a drink with us and talk to her after you've calmed down."

Jameson motioned to their server.

Saxon's shoulders slumped. He might as well have a drink.

Drumming his fingers on the table, he waited for his bourbon. As soon as the server placed it in front of him, he downed it in one gulp. His mind was racing, trying to come up with a plan to find Lovie and Tarik. He could call Sloane and ask her where Tarik lived, but he knew talking to Sloane would only piss him off more.

Jameson and Noemie tried to make small talk, but Saxon barely registered what they were saying. He was too focused on his thoughts.

Saxon signaled for another drink and downed it even quicker than the first. The burn of the alcohol did nothing to ease his mind. He couldn't shake the image of Lovie with Tarik out of his head. He felt like he'd lost her already. She'd said they were done but he hadn't really believed that. He knew she was fuming when she'd said it but he hoped when tempers calmed, they'd be able to talk about things.

Lovie moving on with Tarik, of all people, wasn't part of the plan.

A growl rumbled in his chest, and he slammed his glass down on the table with enough force to make Noemie jump.

"Sorry," Saxon muttered, running his hand over his face. "What am I supposed to do?"

Noemie placed a gentle hand on his arm. "You can call her in the morning, ask her if she'd be willing to meet for coffee then you two can talk things out."

Saxon scoffed. "That's easier said than done."

Jameson leaned forward, his eyes fixed on Saxon. "You need to think logically. We know Tarik is guilty. Did you tell Lovie he was the one who broke into your store?"

Saxon shook his head. He hadn't had a chance to tell her any of the recent developments.

"Then maybe she doesn't know the whole story," Noemie suggested, her voice soft and soothing. "Maybe she's just trying to find out more information."

Saxon ran a hand through his hair. "But why with Tarik?" he asked, his voice rising. "Why not come to me?"

Jameson leaned back in his seat. "Maybe she's trying to protect you. She knows how you feel about him and she doesn't want to add fuel to the fire."

Saxon rubbed the back of his neck, feeling frustrated and helpless. He didn't want to lose Lovie, but he also didn't want to be in a situation where he was constantly worrying about her.

Noemie urged Saxon to eat something and they ordered wings to snack on as they talked. Once the food was gone, Noemie and Jameson decided to head home.

The night air was cool and refreshing as the trio left the Boot Scoot.

Jameson turned to Saxon. "Are you ok to drive? Maybe you should come home with us and crash on the couch for a few hours."

Saxon shook his head. "I'm ok. Thanks though." He didn't feel any better than he had before he arrived, but at least he had a clearer head. He would call Lovie in the morning and see if they could meet up for coffee.

He would tell her why he had to cancel Sloane's book signing and ask her to give them another chance. He would tell her he was falling for her.

As he climbed into his SUV, he couldn't help but feel a nagging sense of doubt. What if Lovie really had moved on? What if she was seeing Tarik and he couldn't do anything about it?

After putting on his seat belt, Saxon sat, staring out at the inky dark sky. He should be heading home but the thought of the empty space made him sigh deeply. He missed coming home to someone. No, check that. He missed coming home to someone who actually wanted to see him. At the end of their marriage, he'd dreaded walking in the door to Sloane's complaints that inevitably led to arguments and then stony silence.

Saxon started the engine and flipped on the heater. The night was unusually chilly and he hadn't bothered with a jacket when he'd stormed out of his place.

The interior warmed quickly and Saxon's eyelids got heavy. He hadn't had much sleep since the break in and the warm air coupled with the bourbon in his belly lulled him into resting his head on the steering wheel.

Saxon was startled awake by a loud noise that sounded like an explosion. His heart raced as he looked around. The parking lot was empty except for his SUV. He rubbed his eyes, trying to get them to focus in the darkness. A glance at the clock on his dashboard showed it was just after two in the morning.

His gut twisted with dread. He put the SUV into gear and drove out of the parking lot, his heart pounding in his chest. The streets were empty except for a few parked cars along the sides.

As he neared his store, a fire truck raced past and he could see the faint glow of flames rising up into the night sky.

Saxon heart pounded as he took the scene in.

His beloved bookstore was engulfed in flames.

He recalled Sloane's words.

I told them to burn it down, you know.

He slammed the palm of his hand against the steering wheel. This had to be all Tarik's doing. Sloane's words raced through his brain.

So you could feel what it's like to have something you love taken from you.

Saxon quickly pulled over to the side of the street and jumped out of his SUV. He ran towards the burning building, but the heat was too intense, forcing him to step back. The sound of shattering glass and crackling wood filled his ears.

All the hard work and passion he'd put into the store over the years were now reduced to ashes. Tears stung his eyes as he thought about the countless hours he'd spent in the store, surrounded by the smell of books and the sense of calm that only reading could provide.

Saxon's heart raced as he watched his dream go up in smoke.

It was all gone now.

Saxon fell to his knees, his chest heaving with sobs. He didn't know how long he stayed there, alone in the dark, watching his life's work burn. A tentative hand on his shoulder jolted him out of his thoughts.

"Saxon..." Lovie kneeled near him. She sniffed. "I am so sorry, I tried to get here in time once I figured out what Tarik was up to but I was too late."

Saxon's heart skipped a beat at the sound of Lovie's voice. He turned his head and saw her kneeling beside him, tears streaming down her face. He couldn't believe she was there, with him, in his darkest moment. He didn't know what to say.

He stood and helped her to her feet.

Lovie placed a gentle hand on his cheek, wiping away his tears. "I'm so glad you weren't in the building. I kept calling and when you didn't pick up, I feared the worst. I thought I'd lost you."

Saxon grimaced. "I raced to the Boot Scoot to confront you and Tarik; I left my phone on the counter in the apartment."

"Saxon, I would never...I was out with Tarik to get him to confess. I didn't want him."

Saxon looked at her, his eyes searching hers for any signs of deception. But all he saw was raw emotion, genuine remorse, and a hint of fear. Fear of losing him, maybe? He couldn't be sure. But in that moment, he didn't care. He needed her.

"I'm sorry...for so much," he murmured, pulling her into a fierce hug.

He leaned forward and captured her lips with his, pouring all his pent-up emotions into the kiss. Lovie responded eagerly, her fingers caressing his face as she deepened the kiss. Saxon pulled her closer, reveling in the feel of her body against his.

Saxon heard a throat clearing behind him. Slowly he released Lovie and turned to face Sheriff Robbie Boyd.

"Saxon, a word?"

Saxon nodded as Lovie squeezed his hand in support.

He followed the sheriff a few feet away from Lovie, his heart still racing from the kiss.

"What's going on, Sheriff?" Saxon asked, his voice heavy with emotion.

"We caught one of the men responsible for the fire," Boyd said, his tone somber. "As soon as we nabbed him, he confessed and implicated Tarik and your ex-wife hoping to make a deal for a lesser sentence. Tarik's in custody now too. And we understand that Sloane is being held for questioning in Louisville."

Saxon felt a sense of relief wash over him. Finally, Tarik was caught, and justice would be served. He hoped that he would never have to see Tarik or Sloane again. But then, a sense of sadness overcame him as he thought about what he had lost.

"My store is gone," Saxon said, his voice breaking. "Everything I've worked for, it's all gone."

Boyd laid a hand on Saxon's shoulder. "I'm sorry, Saxon. Everyone in town will feel this loss. We love your store and we're here to help. Whatever you need."

Saxon nodded, feeling grateful for the sheriff's words. But he couldn't shake the feeling of loss. He had poured his heart and soul into that bookstore and now it was all gone.

As he turned to walk back to Lovie, he wondered what he would do now. He didn't have a store to run, but he couldn't imagine doing anything else.

He approached Lovie. "Thank you for being here."

She studied him. "I couldn't imagine being anywhere else right now. Where are you going to stay?"

He hadn't thought about that. The flames hadn't appeared to destroy his apartment but he wouldn't know how much water damage there was until the fire was completely out.

"I can stay with my aunt and uncle, or Jameson and his wife, I guess. I think I'll be ok."

She sighed and looked away, seeming to get shy on him. "Would you want to come stay in a vacation house with a couple of women and two girls with endless energy? We could use someone to entertain all their questions."

Saxon considered her offer. He didn't want to impose, but he didn't relish the idea of being alone in his aunt and uncle's guest room either. And the thought of being around Lovie and her family was a comfort.

"I would like that," he said, offering her a half smile.

Lovie beamed and hugged him tightly. "Great! We have plenty

of room. And don't worry about anything - we'll take care of you."

Saxon felt a warmth spread through his chest at her words. He didn't know what the future held, but he knew that he had Lovie by his side. And that was enough for now.

As they made their way back to their cars, Saxon kept stealing glances at her. He thought about her often in the days since the break-in, but he never expected to see her again. And now, she was offering him a place to stay. He wondered what had changed.

"Lovie, can I ask you something?" He watched as she pulled the car handle to unlock her car.

"Of course," she said, turning to look at him.

He hesitated. "Why were you out with Tarik? When Jameson called and told me you were out with him, I nearly lost it. I know you said we were through but I never expected you to run to him."

"I went out with him hoping he'd confide in me about the break-in." Lovie tugged him toward her then took his hands in hers. "Jameson saw us leaving and confronted him with what Sloane confessed and Tarik couldn't wait to leave. I followed him and found out he was having his partner set everything in motion to burn down the store. I tried to call you and warn you, but when you didn't answer and I heard the explosion, I thought the worst." She shook her head. "I was too late to stop them."

He pulled her to him. "No, Lovie, you're the reason the fire wasn't worse. And since you called 911 so quickly, they were able to catch Tarik and his partner. You saved the day."

He kissed her then, trying to convey all the love he had for her in his heart.

"I love you, Lovie Whitfield," he whispered against her lips.

"I love you too, Saxon," she replied, pulling him in for another kiss. "Let's go home."

CHAPTER 16

Lovie

The sun was rising as Lovie pulled up to the vacation house with Saxon in tow. After answering questions from the investigators and trying unsuccessfully to salvage some of Saxon's things, they were finally able to head in for some much needed rest.

But Lovie doubted she'd be able to sleep. Her nerves threatened to overwhelm her. It wasn't like her to bring a man home, especially not so soon after their reconciliation. But she knew that she wanted Saxon to be a part of her life and her family's life. And she hoped they would accept him with open arms.

The kids, Jasmine and Jeneva, were wide awake and waiting for them. They ran up to Lovie, hugging her tightly while bombarding her with questions.

"Auntie Love, are you okay?" Jasmine asked, her big brown eyes filled with concern.

"We heard about the explosion," Jeneva chimed in. "Was it loud? Did the fire truck come?"

Lovie smiled at the girls, knowing they'd have a ton of questions. "I'm okay now, sweethearts. Luckily no one was hurt."

The girls turned their attention to Saxon, their eyes wide with curiosity. "Who's he?" Jasmine whispered loudly, crooking a thumb at Saxon.

"This is Mr. Saxon," Lovie said, introducing him to her nieces. "He's a friend."

Saxon smiled at the girls, his eyes twinkling with amusement. "Friend of your Auntie Love's," he said, winking at Lovie.

Jasmine cocked her head to one side, looking just like Layla. "Is this your boyfriend, Auntie Love?"

Lovie couldn't meet Saxon's eye. She wasn't quite ready to announce anything like that.

Saxon knelt down to Jasmine's level. "I would like to be Auntie Love's boyfriend, if that's ok with you?"

Brow furrowed, Jasmine seemed to contemplate the question. "We'll have to see what you can make for breakfast. We like pancakes. Can you make pancakes?"

Saxon lifted a brow, looking at Lovie. "I can. How about chocolate chip pancakes?"

Layla, in a robe fancier than Lovie had ever seen on her sister, appeared then. "Jas, you're not supposed to demand our guests make breakfast. Your aunt needs a nap, so let's go find something to do."

She turned to Saxon. "Sorry about that. You don't have to make them pancakes. I'm Layla by the way."

"Yes, he does, Mommy! He wants to be Auntie Love's boyfriend and boyfriends should make pancakes." Jasmine crossed her arms.

"Jas, I'm gonna count to three..."

Jasmine scurried off toward her bedroom.

Lovie bit her lip to keep from laughing as she and Saxon watched the girls disappear down the hall before turning back to each other.

"Nice to meet you, Layla," Saxon said, shaking her hand. "I've heard a lot about you."

"Same," Layla said. "I'm sorry about your store. The girls loved the books you suggested."

Saxon nodded. "Thanks."

Layla clasped her hands together, "Well, I know you two have had an eventful evening and need some rest, so I'll take the girls out for a while."

With that she disappeared down the hall again and Lovie turned to Saxon with a wry smile on her face.

"So yeah," she said, "that went well."

Saxon chuckled and took a step toward her, his deep brown eyes twinkling in amusement. "It certainly did," he said softly, caressing her cheek with his thumb.

Lovie felt warmth wash over her skin as their eyes locked in the dark hallway. She could see all the possibilities of what their future could hold reflected back at her from his gaze - and it made her heart swell with anticipation.

Then she remembered where they were standing - in the middle of the living room - and stepped back abruptly, shaking herself out of the moment.

Layla and the girls, dressed for the park, appeared. "Ok, we're gone. Text me if you want something from the store. We'll grab breakfast while we're out."

The girls charged out of the front door. "You two kids have fun," Layla threw a knowing look at Lovie.

Lovie waved at her sister then turned to Saxon. "There are bunk beds in the basement," she pointed toward the door leading downstairs. "Or you can share my room."

"Hmm...I should probably take the bunk bed. But," he said, running a slow hand up her arm that sent chills racing through her, "I really want Auntie Love to read me a bedtime story."

Lovie's heart skipped a beat as Saxon leaned in closer to her. His warm breath fanned across her neck, sending electric shocks through her body.

"I can do that," she whispered back, her voice slightly shaky. "But only if you promise to behave yourself."

Saxon grinned devilishly. "Oh, I'll behave," he said, his eyes sparkling with mischief.

Lovie rolled her eyes, a smile playing at the corners of her lips. "Come on then," she said, leading him to the master bedroom. "Let's get you to bed."

She made a beeline to her suitcase and pulled out a t-shirt. "I know you gave this to me when I spent the night but you can wear it."

Saxon held the logoed shirt up to his nose. "Well, now it smells like you so maybe I'll take it back."

She shook her head. "I love that shirt so I'm just loaning it to you." Lovie looked around. "Unfortunately, I don't have any shorts that will fit you."

Saxon shrugged. "This is more than I usually wear. But I'm realizing that I don't have anything. Everything I own is in that apartment or the store."

Lovie felt a pang of empathy for Saxon. She knew how important his store was to him and how devastating it was to watch it succumb to the fire. But she also knew that he was a survivor, and she would be there for him every step of the way.

"You'll find a way," she said reassuringly. "We'll figure it out together."

He nodded, giving her a grateful smile. "I want a shower before I turn in, if that's alright with you."

"Of course," Lovie said, gesturing towards the en suite bathroom. "Towels are in the cabinet, and there's shampoo and soap in the shower."

Saxon nodded and disappeared into the bathroom, leaving Lovie alone in the bedroom. She took a deep breath, trying to steady her racing heart. She wanted to make him feel as welcome as he'd made her feel when she'd spent that first night with him.

She peeled off her dress and dropped her shoes in the closet then debated on what she should put on. Her normal cotton night shirt seemed too casual but she also didn't want to presume anything. The man had just lost his home and livelihood in one night. Sex was probably the last thing on his mind.

She was still standing in her bra and panties when the

bathroom door opened. Saxon emerged, his body glistening with moisture, a towel wrapped around his waist.

Lovie's breath caught in her throat at the sight of him and she couldn't remember her name right at that moment. Lovie knew what those broad shoulders and chiseled chest felt like against her heated skin. She could feel her body responding to him, desire pooling low in her belly.

Saxon walked towards her, his eyes full of hunger. "You've got on my favorite outfit."

Lovie's heart raced as he leaned in to kiss her. His lips were soft and warm, and she melted into him. She ran her fingers through his damp hair, pulling him closer. Saxon's hands found their way to her hips, pulling her towards him.

Their kiss deepened as Saxon's tongue traced the outline of Lovie's lips. She opened her mouth, allowing him to explore her further. His touch was electric, and she couldn't get enough of him. Lovie moaned as Saxon's hands roamed her body, exploring every inch of her.

Finally breaking the kiss, Saxon looked deep into Lovie's eyes. "I missed you, Lovie," he said, his voice rough with desire as he stroked her bottom lip with his thumb. "I was afraid I'd never get to touch you like this again."

Lovie's heart swelled with love and longing. She had been waiting for this moment for so long. "I missed you too," she said, her voice barely above a whisper. "I thought I lost you."

She exhaled, reliving those moments when Saxon hadn't answered his phone and she'd assumed the unthinkable. Lovie clung to him, desperate to be as close as possible.

Saxon held her face in his hands. "I'm not going anywhere," he said fiercely. "I'm yours - if you'll have me."

He kissed her again, his touch sending shivers of delight through her body. She parted her lips, allowing his tongue to continue exploring the inside of her mouth. Her body responded to his touch with a ferocity that took her breath away.

Lovie wrapped her arms around Saxon's broad shoulders,

loving the feel of his skin against hers. "I'm all yours," she whispered into his ear.

Saxon picked Lovie up and carried her to the bed, his lips never leaving hers. She felt weightless in his arms, her body responding to his touch. Saxon pulled back and gazed at her with an adoration that Lovie had only imagined in her daydreams.

Saxon slowly lowered her onto the bed, hovering over her as he pressed a trail of kisses from her lips down to her chin, then to her neck. Lovie groaned as Saxon's warm tongue found its way to her collar bone and then lower to the valley between her breasts.

Lovie's heart pounded against her chest as Saxon began to trail his fingertips down her body. He slid the cups of her bra down and took her breasts in his hands, teasing the sensitive peaks before trailing his fingers down her stomach. His touch was light and soft, driving her wild with anticipation.

Lovie shivered, trying to keep herself from becoming too impatient. Saxon was taking his time, as if he were savoring the feel of her skin. He trailed his fingers down the inside of her thighs, causing Lovie to lift her hips towards him.

Unable to resist, she reached up and pulled the towel away, revealing his rock-hard erection. Lovie took him in her hand, giving him a gentle stroke. His breath caught in his throat and he pulled her tightly to him.

He trailed kisses down her neck and over the swell of her breasts. Lovie arched her back as Saxon took a nipple in his mouth, suckling her deeply. Lovie moaned at the sensation and she felt a rush of heat between her legs.

Saxon worked his way down her body, teasing and delighting her with every touch. He stopped at the waistline of her panties, pressing his lips along the elastic.

She wanted to shove them down her legs and off, but Lovie forced herself to be patient. They had the house to themselves for a while.

Finally, Saxon tugged her panties down her legs, taking his

time to taste every inch of her skin. When he reached her thighs, he kissed the inside of her right knee, and then her left one.

Lovie reached out for him, wrapping her hands around his neck, trying to draw Saxon closer. Saxon kissed her inner thighs, making her groan in desire. He teased her with the tip of his tongue, kissing her lightly and driving her wild.

Lovie had never been so turned on in her life.

She moaned softly as Saxon held her hips, nipping lightly at her inner thighs before plunging his tongue deep inside her. Her body was on fire, every nerve ending tingling with delight. Saxon brought her to the edge and then pulled her back, repeating the process again and again until she didn't know if she could take much more.

Lovie was panting now and she opened her eyes, reaching for Saxon. He looked up at her, his eyes full of desire. Lovie pulled him up to her, eager to feel every inch of his body against hers. Saxon thrust into her, going deep, filling her completely. She wrapped her legs around his waist, holding him to her.

Saxon rocked his hips against her, his eyes never leaving hers. She could see his desire in his eyes with each of his powerful thrusts. She wrapped her arms around him, holding him tightly, completely lost in the sensation of his touch.

She could feel the pressure building inside her and she closed her eyes to savor the moment. Saxon brushed a strand of her hair away, his breath warm against her ear.

"Open your eyes, Lovie," he whispered. "I want to see you when you come."

Looking deep into Saxon's dark eyes, she could feel her body racing towards the edge. She held on tightly to Saxon as she surrendered to her climax. She closed her eyes as wave after wave of pleasure washed over her, making her whole body quiver deliciously.

When her body finally calmed, Saxon thrust into her one last time. Lovie clung to him as his release came and he exhaled a long sigh of contentment. He ground out her name in her ear, expressing his love for her in the one desperate word. Saxon slumped beside her then pulled her to his chest.

She gazed up at him as they caught their breath. She couldn't believe Saxon was back in her arms.

She sighed a deeply contented sigh. "I love you," she whispered.

Saxon didn't open his eyes. "You better after all that work I just put in," he murmured into her hair.

She pinched his thigh and snuggled into his arms.

Later that day, Lovie awoke to a loud grinding sound. She pushed up onto her elbows and noticed she was alone in the bed. Was that a blender? She jumped up, concerned that the girls were attempting to use the blender unsupervised. She grabbed her robe, tying it tightly and hurrying out of her room.

Chaos reigned in the kitchen.

Saxon was showing Jeneva how to run the blender and Jasmine was licking a beater covered in what she hoped was whipped cream.

Hmm.

Jasmine held up the beater, her mouth white with whipped cream. "Auntie Love! You're finally up! We're having breakfast for dinner! We made pancakes and cream and Mr. Saxon told us to let you sleep in cause you had a long night."

Her eyes slid to Saxon's.

He lifted a shoulder, a satisfied grin on his face.

"You go sit with Mommy and we'll call you when everything's ready," Jasmine stated.

"Yes ma'am." Lovie spied her sister on the screened in porch, sipping from a mug in her hand, and strode out to join her.

"Have they torn up the whole kitchen yet?" Layla asked.

"No idea. I was told to sit out here with you." Lovie took the wicker seat next to her sister.

Layla set her cup down. "Glad you two reconciled."

Lovie's face warmed. "Yeah, you could say that. Thanks for taking the girls out."

Layla smirked. "Anytime. I figured you might need some time alone to sort things out," she winked at Lovie, "all three of them have been waiting for you to get up though. That man really loves you."

Shaking her head, Lovie wouldn't meet her sister's eyes.

"Anyway," Layla continued, "I have news. Guess who got a job offer?"

Lovie's head snapped up. "What? Where? Are you going to take the job? Why didn't you lead with that?"

Layla took a sip from her mug before answering. "I got an offer from Joslin & Associates. They're a real estate law firm and they want me to be their office manager," Layla paused. "The job is here in Kissing Springs and I'm thinking I will take it."

Lovie stared at her sister. "You'd move from Charlotte? Are you sure?"

"Yeah, I mean, we could all live here. What's keeping us in Charlotte? I was staying so the kids could see their dad regularly, but that asshole is moving to Florida, and honestly, I think a new place would be good for the girls. I like this town."

Layla studied her mug. "You and Saxon can see where things go and you've already got some business contacts. I can help you with some of your admin stuff. Think about it."

Lovie watched as Saxon and her nieces set the kitchen table and laid out dishes of food.

Maybe this could work.

Epilogue

"**A**nd this tool here is great," Saxon called the book club's attention to the screen. "So you'll enter your favorite genres here, whether that's mystery or sci-fi or romance then you enter a favorite book or movie and," he tapped the "Go" button with his index finger, "the artificial intelligence tool will compile a list of books you'll love and shows you an exclusive trailer for each. Then you can press "Order" and it will send your order to the register where they'll be ready for you when you want to check out."

The book club, a group of six women in their forties that had taken a road trip from DC to visit his store, started posting about the device and clamoring to try it out.

Saxon felt a rush of pride as he watched the book club try out his AI tool for the first time. It had taken countless hours and lots of trial-and-error, but it was finally ready and in the hands of people who were eager to use a new tool.

One of the women, a tall, curvy blonde with striking green eyes, sauntered over to him. "You running this empire by yourself?

I'm sure you could use a partner. I'm a former bartender and I love books." She winked at him.

As if on cue, Lovie appeared at his side. "No, he's got that covered," she smiled sweetly at the woman, leading her toward the new oak bourbon bar. "Can I interest you in a glass of Kentucky Lemonade? Or are you more of a mint julep kind of woman?"

Saxon grinned, shaking his head. God, he loved that woman.

Lovie mock rolled her eyes at him before turning to the ladies and mixing up the drinks. The curvy blonde asked her a question and she launched into a long explanation of how certain bourbons were better than others.

Saxon pulled out his phone and typed out a quick text.

He watched, amused, as Lovie glanced at her phone, then up at him, her eyebrows raised in puzzlement.

He'd invited her to meet him down in the media room once the store was closed, in about thirty minutes.

He motioned for her to continue her presentation.

She shook her head and pulled out another bottle of bourbon.

Saxon walked around the store, his mind spinning with thoughts of Lovie and all she had accomplished in the last year. Her business was flourishing, and she was doing publicity for some of the best-known authors in the world. After all the news coverage surrounding Sloane's role in the fire and his stolen bourbon collection, a podcaster had done a series about the bourbon black market and curious tourists clamored to visit the store. Then he'd had a number of best-selling authors contact him about doing signings. He'd funneled all of their inquiries to Lovie.

He was extremely proud of her and her success.

But then his mind shifted to the little velvet box in his pocket. He stopped mid-stride, feeling a fluttery sensation in his stomach.

Should he ask her to marry him tonight? His heart raced as he thought about it, but then doubt crept in. Her career was in full swing, why would she want to slow down and get married? She seemed content with things just the way they were.

Maybe he should wait until things slowed down.

No. He shook his head. He couldn't wait that long. When he knew what he wanted, he'd found it was best to go after it.

He was pacing again and caught Lovie staring at him, the concern on her face causing her to frown.

She made her way to him, putting her hand on his arm to stop him from walking back and forth.

"Everything ok? What's going on?" she asked in a shaky voice.

He patted her arm. "Nothing. Just meet me downstairs when everyone leaves. I'll pour us some wine."

She raised an eyebrow. "You sure you're ok? You're not going to tell me you're seeing someone else, are you?"

She chuckled as she said the last part, but Saxon could tell Lovie was on high alert.

"Nope, you're stuck with me." He kissed her forehead. "See you in a bit."

Saxon made his way down to the media room. The space now had a small wine cellar and a soundproof room that he rented to content creators for their podcast recordings.

He checked the time. Fifteen minutes until closing.

Extracting the ring box from his pocket, Saxon popped it open and stared at the ring. The two carat princess cut ring sparkled in the light. This one was less flashy than the ring he'd given Sloane, but he'd put more effort into selecting Lovie's ring. This time around, he'd considered Lovie's style and what she would like. This ring looked like it was made especially for her, at least that's what he hoped. He'd taken Layla ring shopping with him when he finally narrowed down his choices and she'd chosen the one he preferred.

Now he just needed Lovie to say yes.

He snapped the ring box shut and shoved it back in his pocket.

It was time.

Saxon tested the video and adjusted the sound.

He glanced at his watch. The store had just closed and Lovie would be heading his way any moment now.

Saxon took a deep breath, feeling a mixture of nerves and excitement coursing through his veins. He heard footsteps approaching the door and his heart skipped a beat.

"Lovie, come in!" he called out, his voice betraying none of the nervousness he felt.

The door opened and Lovie stepped in, her eyes widening in surprise at the sight of Daphne on the screen. "Hey, what's going on?" she asked, her eyes flickering to the bottle of Bordeaux and the tray of glasses on the table.

Saxon motioned for her to come closer, and she walked over to stand next to him. "Lovie, Daphne from our first wine tasting recorded a video for us." he said, gesturing towards the screen.

Lovie smiled. "That was nice of her. What's the occasion? "

Saxon poured them each a glass of wine and handed one to Lovie. He used the remote to start the video.

Daphne spoke. "This is a new wine from our winery. It's a Bordeaux Blanc made from blending Sémillon and Sauvignon Blanc. These wines represent the perfect union of the grape blends, much like the perfect union between two people in love."

Lovie looked at Saxon, her head tilted to the side. "Is there a reason for this impromptu wine tasting?" she asked, taking a sip of the wine. "Wow, that's amazing."

Her eyes lit up. "Are you finally going to start offering wine tastings?"

Saxon took a deep breath, his heart beating so fast he thought it might burst out of his chest. "Umm...not yet. But, there is a reason for this tasting," he said, pulling the small velvet box out of his pocket.

Lovie's eyes widened as he got down on one knee in front of her. She put her glass down and covered her mouth with her hands.

"Lovie Whitfield, I love you more than anything in this world.

Since that first day you strutted into my store you've brought so much light and love into my life. I can't imagine living another day without you by my side. Will you marry me?"

For a moment, Lovie just stared at him, her eyes wide with shock. Then, tears welled up in her eyes and she took a deep breath. "One question," she picked up her wine glass. "Can we serve this at the wedding?"

"We can serve whatever you want." Saxon opened the ring box, waiting for her answer.

"Then my answer is yes," she said, her voice shaking with emotion.

Saxon slipped the ring onto her finger, his heart bursting with happiness. He stood up, pulling Lovie into his arms and kissing her deeply.

As they broke apart, Lovie looked down at the ring on her finger and then up at Saxon. "It's beautiful," she said, her voice full of awe.

Saxon grinned from ear to ear. "I'm glad you like it. Layla said you would."

"She was in on this too? She didn't say a word." Lovie wiggled her left hand.

"I swore her to secrecy."

They watched a few minutes more of the video with Daphne explaining more about the white wine they were drinking then the video ended.

Saxon led Lovie over to the couch, grabbing his own glass of Bordeaux and settling in next to her. "I've been planning this for a while now," he said, taking a deep sip of the wine. "I wanted it to be special."

"It was," Lovie said, leaning into him. "I feel so loved."

"You are," Saxon replied, wrapping his arm around her and pulling her closer. "And I can't wait to spend the rest of my life with you."

"If someone had told me I'd find love in a small town with a cranky bookstore owner, I'd have thrown my head back and laughed hard. But here I am."

"Same. Who knew the annoyingly happy woman blowing up my phone and email would turn out to be the best thing to happen to me since I discovered bourbon?"

Lovie rolled her eyes.

They sat in companionable silence for a few minutes, sipping their wine and enjoying each other's presence. Finally, Saxon spoke up. "You know, I was thinking, I've learned a lot about wine, Bordeaux especially, all thanks to you."

"Yeah, you swore bourbon was the only thing you'd ever drink and look at you now." She swirled her wine, giving him that "I told you so" look he'd come to know well.

"Anyway, I was thinking we could spend our honeymoon in France...go to Bordeaux and source some wines for the store while we're there."

Lovie's eyes widened in excitement. "That sounds amazing, Saxon. I'd love that."

Saxon grinned, feeling a sense of relief that she was on board with his idea. "I figured we could stay in a chateau, do some wine tastings, and just enjoy each other's company. What do you think?"

"I think it sounds perfect," Lovie said, leaning up to kiss him on the lips. "I can't wait."

Saxon felt a sense of contentment wash over him, knowing that he had found the love of his life and that they had a bright future together. He raised his glass in a toast. "To us," he said.

"To us," Lovie repeated, clinking her glass with his.

The End

~

Love this story? Please leave a review on Goodreads or your favorite retailer.
To get exclusive access to bonus scenes and a prequel, visit the Purple Peacock Press (www.purplepeacockpress.com) site.

Visit my Facebook page!

Read the story that started it all, Silver Santa

Silver Santa

A single dad gym owner with a newly empty nest. A strait-laced guidance counselor with one birthday wish.

This Christmas, a steamy second chance romance twenty years in the making is about to ignite.

Happily divorced high school guidance counselor Noemie Saint has moved back to Kissing Springs to be closer to her mother after her father's death. She wouldn't say she's avoiding the ex that broke her heart twenty years ago, but she's certainly not going out of her way to run into him.

Twenty years ago, he chose to do the right thing and let Noemie go. Now that she's moved back to town and they are both single, he's sure he can convince her they belong together.

She wants one night, he wants forever. Can this second chance couple make some Christmas magic?

Read Jameson's sister Gia's story

Sunshine & Silk Boxers

Gia and Winston's friendship is tested when Gia discovers Dre, her one-night stand from Nashville, has moved to Kissing Springs. With both men vying for her heart, will Gia choose her best friend or take a chance with a younger man?

This is a love triangle, age gap story that will set your summer ablaze!
Buy now using the QR code below!

Welcome to Kissing Springs

MULTI-AUTHOR STEAMY ROMANCE SERIES

Welcome to Kissing Springs, Kentucky!

In this new collection of steamy romance, multiple authors bring you standalone stories from single dads to second chances, ex-military to sports romances all set in the small town of Kissing Springs, Kentucky.

Santa Season:

Welcome to Kissing Springs

Sunshine Season:

Welcome to Kissing Springs: Sunshine Season

Bourbon Season:

Welcome to Kissing Springs: Bourbon Season

The Love, Lies, and Catfish Series

Book 1

To Catch a Catfish

Research analyst London Lewis's first online dating investigation should have been a piece of cake.

Regardless of how cute and charming she found her first client, she should have maintained a professional relationship with him.

Plot twist: It wasn't and she didn't.

Book 2

Catfish in Paradise

Coming in 2024

www.ingramcontent.com/pod-product-compliance
Lightning Source LLC
Chambersburg PA
CBHW061543310726
48972CB00008B/2591